Snarl

A Kate Redman Mystery: Book 4

Celina Grace

Prologue

ON THE LAST MORNING OF his life, Michael Frank forgot to kiss his wife goodbye. It was a simple omission, brought about by the worse than usual morning chaos and the knowledge that if he didn't get a move on, he'd be late for his nine o'clock meeting. Knowing that next year's research budget hinged on the successful outcome of this particular meeting, Michael was rather more harried than usual.

Mary Frank was preoccupied with unloading the dishwasher, trying to find the second of her older son's football boots and chivvying both her children into brushing their teeth, rather than watching the television, which was currently blaring out from the corner of the living room, in total disregard of the usual morning dictate of 'no TV before everyone's ready' rule.

"I'm off," Michael said, grabbing his briefcase and doing his best to straighten his hastily-tied tie with his one free hand. "Have you seen the car keys?"

"Wherever you put them last," snapped Mary, crashing the door of the dishwasher shut. "Kids! Would you get a bloody move on?"

Michael found the keys on the third hook by the front door; not the first hook, where they *should* have been. Muttering, he picked up his briefcase again, called a goodbye to his children, who were finally heading upstairs to the bathroom, and another to his wife before pulling the front door closed behind him.

Cut off from the tumult, he took a deep breath, savouring the momentary peace. The Franks had not long moved to the house in Polton Winter, shortly after Michael started his new job at the MedGen Research Facility. Michael walked down the drive to his car, next to a young beech tree, newly clothed in fresh, bright green leaves. Michael unlocked the car, flung his briefcase in the passenger seat and, catching sight of the time on his wristwatch, cursed. His lateness made him just a little bit less cautious than he normally was and he jumped into the driver's seat and jammed the key into the ignition, turning it swiftly on.

The explosion, as the device clamped to the underside of the suspension ignited, was the loudest thing ever heard in the sleepy little hamlet of Polton Winter. The car blossomed into a firework display of debris as the fireball tore through it, hurling twisted pieces of metal, lethal shards of glass and smoking body parts into the air. Michael's forearm was flung against the front wall of the house, as if knocking for entry. Fortunately, Mary Frank had bent down to continue unloading the dishwasher as the front windows of the house shattered into thousands of pieces, and she escaped the worst of the blast. The two Frank children were closeted in the bathroom at the back of the house, but as the explosion roared like an angry dragon, they dropped the foamy brushes from their mouths and screamed in utter terror.

As the noise faded to the crackle of the flames that remained, and people in the village began to stream from their houses, drawn towards the oily smoke and the tick-tick-tick of cooling metal, blackened wisps of the beech tree's leaves began to sift down from the sky, like the singed feathers of a million little birds.

Chapter One

KATE REDMAN FACED HER REFLECTION in the mirror by the front door. Hair smooth and fringe neat – check. Jacket settled squarely on her shoulders – check. She was annoyed to find her hands were shaking a little and she flexed her fingers, straightening them out and trying to stem their trembling. She checked her bag: purse, phone and warrant card, all present and correct.

Kate wandered through to the living room, peered out the window and then let the curtain fall back into place. He was late, although not by much. She went back to her station by the front door, regarding herself in the mirror again. Her return-to-work outfit had been carefully chosen. She wanted to look composed, firm and no-nonsense, not a hint of the invalid about her. Automatically, her hand went to the small of her back, pressing against the raised ridge of the scar beneath her ribcage. Where the hell was he? He knew she'd be nervous so, just *for once*, why couldn't he be on time? Kate tried to slow her breathing, consciously bringing the air deep into her lungs, aware that her chest was tightening up.

As if on cue, the doorbell rang and she jumped. Grabbing her bag, she pinched the bridge of her nose, closed her eyes momentarily and took another deep breath. She adjusted her face – she wanted to get her expression and tone just right. Then she flung the door back with a beaming smile.

"Good morning, Detective Inspector Olbeck."

Olbeck smiled, a little sheepishly. "Morning. Sorry I'm late."

"I'm used to it, Detective Inspector."

"How are you feeling?"

Kate wondered whether she could push it a third time and decided, what the hell, she would anyway. "I'm fine, thanks, Detective Inspector."

"All right, all right," said Olbeck, grinning. "You've made your point. I don't hear any congratulations, by the way."

"I *said* congratulations when you told me," said Kate, locking her front door. Now that Olbeck was actually here, she felt better. It was always the way – anticipation was the worst thing, reality was never quite as bad. In almost all cases.

"Feel free to say it again," said Olbeck, ushering her to the passenger seat. "As many times as you like."

"Nope," retorted Kate, buckling up. "That's your lot."

"Oh well." Olbeck slammed the driver-side door and started the engine. "Thanks for the card, seriously. It was nice."

"You're welcome."

Kate watched the sunny streets of Abbeyford roll past as they drove on for a few moments in companionable silence. Kate watched the flicker of blue sky visible between the roofs and walls of the buildings flashing by the windows. It was late spring; warm, sunny, with the full glory of the spring flowers and tree blossom in evidence.

"How are you feeling?" Olbeck asked.

"Fine."

He glanced over at her. "No, how are you *really* feeling?"

"I'm fine," snapped Kate, her tone belying her words. Olbeck said nothing but hummed a little tune as he indicated to turn right onto the police station road. There was a moment of silence.

"All right," said Kate, giving in. "I'm feeling a bit nervous. It's my first day back, what do you expect?"

"I didn't expect anything," said Olbeck, mildly. He slowed for the entrance to the underground car park beneath the station. "You're bound to be feeling a bit shaken up. I don't blame you."

"Hmm." Kate realised she was clenching her fists and forced herself to relax her hands.

"Did Anderton call you last night?" asked Olbeck.

"No," said Kate. She shot a sideways glance at him. "Why – why, did he say he would?"

"I thought so. Perhaps he meant to and got caught up. Things are a bit hectic at the moment, as I'm sure you can appreciate."

"When aren't they?" murmured Kate.

The station itself hadn't changed. Built sometime in the late sixties, it personified that charmless, boxy style so characteristic of the era: small windows, flat red brick and no features of architectural interest whatsoever. But it was functional, large enough to cope with everything that the Abbeyford criminals could muster between them, and the team's main office had been renovated last year.

Olbeck parked the car and he and Kate got out. Now that they were actually on site, Kate felt her nervousness increasing. That remark of Olbeck's about Anderton phoning her – when he hadn't – had thrown her. She hadn't spoken to Anderton for more than a month, but she'd thought about him every day.

"Got your card?"

Kate groped for her handbag and then remembered. "It expired. I'll have to get Security to give me a new one."

"No probs." Olbeck passed his security card in

front of the door scanner and the door lock clicked back. "In you go."

Kate stepped into the dingy corridor. It smelt the same; disinfectant, photocopier fluid, cooking smells from the canteen. She felt her hands go up, smoothing her hair again with fluttering fingers.

They walked past the door to the cells, up the stairs, past the door to the reception area, up another flight of stairs and along the corridor to the office. Kate let her feet guide her there automatically, her hand trailing up the banister of the stairs. Every so often, there was a little spike of surprise; *oh, that wall's been painted; oh, that poster's new*. She paused at the entrance to the office, unobtrusively, she hoped. Olbeck squeezed her arm and opened the door for her.

The whole team was in the office, it seemed. There was a moment of silence, as everyone clocked who was back, and then a cry of 'Kate!' from Theo, who leapt up from his desk and hurried over, flinging his arms around her. She blushed, pleased and embarrassed. Rav got up from his chair, smiling and waving. Kate's gaze flickered over the desk next to Rav's – she thought of it as 'Jerry's desk', but of course, Jerry was no longer here, having retired last year.

By now, Rav and Jane had come up to say hello and there were slightly awkward hugs and cheek kisses and rather facile chat about how well Kate was looking, how they'd missed her, how was she finding it and was she back for good? Kate said *thanks*, and *me too*, and *not too bad*, and *yes, I hope so*; noting Jane's new haircut, the bountiful red curls shorn off into a rather unforgiving pixie cut; that Rav finally looked a little bit older and not so much like a sixth-former doing some work experience; Theo's sharp new suit, clearly the proceeds of his recent promotion. That last thought struck her rather unpleasantly. Theo, once her subordinate, was now her equal and Olbeck... Olbeck was her superior. Kate smiled more widely to hide the jab that thought gave her, and caught sight of the biggest change yet. Someone else was sat at her desk.

Kate felt the fixed smile drop from her face. Her principal feeling was one of outrage. It wasn't just that there was someone else sitting at her desk. It wasn't just that this person had their chair – Kate's chair – tipped back and their feet propped on the surface of the desk, as if they were relaxing at home on the sofa. It wasn't just that this person was dressed as no detective should ever be dressed: in a filthy T-shirt and combat trousers, falling apart trainers with trailing laces and sporting matted dreadlocks that reached their shoulders. It was all of these things together.

Olbeck had followed Kate's intent gaze. "Ah, yes," he said, taking her arm and pulling her forward.

"Come and meet the newest member of the team. Stuart Granger, meet Kate Redman."

Stuart flipped his dirty shoes off the desk and stood up, extending a large hand to Kate. "Hi," he said, grinning. "You probably shouldn't call me Stuart, though."

"What should I call you?" asked Kate politely, running through a few choice epithets in her head.

"Ah, yes," said Olbeck again. "Stuart's our undercover. He'll be working with the various groups we've got picked out as the possible suspects for the bombing."

Well, that explained the outfit. There was something about his expression, though, that made Kate's hackles rise. What was the word? Self-satisfied? Arrogant? God knows, Kate was used to working with cocky young men, but this Stuart Granger, or whatever the hell he was called, took the biscuit. Perhaps all undercover officers were like that, by nature of the job; she wouldn't know, she hadn't met one before.

Well, you think you haven't, Kate. If they were working undercover, how would you actually know?

"Nice to meet you," said Kate, in a tone barely above freezing. Stuart winked, clearly not upset at her frostiness. She supposed he was quite good looking, in a kind of broad-faced, sandy-haired, cheeky-grin sort of way. She bet he knew it, too.

"So, where am I sitting?" Kate demanded of

Olbeck. It was bad enough having to come back after six months, knowing that everyone was wondering whether you'd be able to hack it again, without being booted off your own desk as well... She knew she was being prickly and defensive but somehow wasn't able to snap herself out of her mood.

"Tell you what," said Olbeck. "You can sit here." He gestured to the desk opposite Stuart.

Kate stared at it and then stared back at him. "That's yours," she said, waiting for the grin and the joke that she was sure was coming.

Olbeck looked a little embarrassed. "Ah," he said. "Not anymore. I'm over there now."

Kate looked at where he gestured. 'There' was a glassed-in cubicle at the end of the room. An office. Olbeck had his own office.

Quickly, before everyone could see, Kate resettled her face and said, in an arch tone "Ooh. Get you!"

"Fancy, huh?" said Olbeck. "I'll even give you the secret password, so you'll be able to enter its hallowed portals."

"You're too kind," said Kate, pulling out the chair from Olbeck's old desk. "Don't let me keep you, Detective Inspector Olbeck." For a moment Olbeck looked at her anxiously and she managed a grin and wink. Clearly relieved, he winked back.

Slowly, everyone settled back to whatever they had been doing before Kate arrived. Kate, left alone, stared blankly at her computer screen. She'd expected to be a bit unsettled, being back here with the team, but for a moment she was afraid that she'd actually start crying. Sitting there, she felt as if all her hard-won knowledge and experience were running away from her, pooling under the unfamiliar desk. What was left wouldn't be enough to sustain her. Sitting at this desk – Olbeck's desk! – with her erstwhile partner ensconced in solitary splendour at the other end of the room made Kate wonder how she was going to get through the rest of the *day*, let alone anything more. How was she going to talk over cases without Olbeck being right there in front of her? Instead, she would have to knock on his office door and request an interview. He's my superior now, she thought again, and her entire middle section felt hollow.

And where the hell was Anderton? Hadn't he heard she was here, and if he had, where was he? Kate continued to look blankly at her computer screen, seeing nothing. Anderton. Her boss. The enigmatic, energetic Chief Inspector, who she had slept with once during the serial killing case last year; an incident apparently relegated to the dim and distant past by both of them. It had never happened again. And I'm glad about that, Kate told herself stoutly. Shagging your boss was no way to progress in your career, despite what some cynics might say.

So it was a bit of a surprise that, when Anderton did finally appear, Kate's stomach seemed to drop floorwards and remain somewhere down by her ankles. On top of that sensation came an unexpected surge of fury. Why hadn't he telephoned her last night, as he had apparently said he would? Why hadn't he come to welcome her back, personally?

He crashed through the door of the incident room as he always did, sending the usual ripples of reaction through the room. People sat up straighter, put their phones down, and turned to face him.

"Morning team, morning team. How are we all, this bright, sunny morning?"

There were a few chuckles and murmurs of assent. Then Anderton caught sight of Kate.

His face flickered minutely, some kind of emotional reaction, gone too swiftly for Kate to interpret it. Then he was smiling, walking forward to greet her. "DS Redman, how long have you been here? You should have come and said hello. How are you?"

"Fine, sir," said Kate, smiling until she thought her face would crack under the strain. "Just getting this lot back into some sort of order."

"God knows they need it," Anderton said. There was an 'Oy' from Theo and a giggle from Jane. "Well, you're looking well. Fit and healthy again."

"I'm fine."

"I've no doubt. Anyway, we'd better get on.

Come and see me after the debrief and we'll catch up properly."

Kate was sure her face was now permanently stuck in this ridiculous smile. She nodded, unable to say anything. Anderton had already turned and was heading back to the front of the room, where the crime scene whiteboards were located. Kate hadn't even had a chance to look at them yet.

Anderton began pacing up and down as the team swung their chairs to keep him in view.

"Now, I'll do a brief recap, for Kate's benefit," he began. "Kate, I'll go into things more thoroughly later, but this is just to get you up to speed so we won't waste any time. As you no doubt know, we're investigating the murder of Doctor Michael Frank, the head of research at the newly opened MedGen Research Facility in Polton. He was killed by an explosive device attached to the underside of his car, which ignited when he started the engine. Your common or garden car bomb, in fact. We've got experts examining what was left of the device – and the car – and we're expecting the full report back in a couple of days. Suffice to say, they reckon it was made by an amateur, but one with a sufficient knowledge of explosives to produce a device that actually works. Which it undoubtedly did."

Anderton reached the far side of the office, turned on his heel and began to pace back again. Kate couldn't help a small smile. He didn't change;

he still prowled about the room like a caged tiger. She wondered if you strapped Anderton in a chair and forced him to deliver his debrief completely stationary, whether he'd be struck dumb. Then she blinked and made an effort to switch her thoughts. The thought of Anderton strapped to a chair was provoking some highly unprofessional feelings.

"As you know, the opening of the MedGen research facility has resulted in a lot of negative press attention, protest groups and demonstrations. There's been the kind of civil disorder you'd expect from this kind of event, but I'm not sure we could have anticipated that the stakes would rise quite so highly or quickly. This is an act of terrorism, make no mistake. The people who did this will most probably attempt the same thing again, if they think it's been effective in fighting their cause. We need to make sure that they don't get the chance."

Anderton came to a halt by a convenient desk and hoisted himself onto it.

"I've been consulting with a few bods from Counter Terrorism Command, up at The Met, to get some background on the types of groups that might do this. I'm hopeful that one of them might deign to come down and give a face to face rundown of what we can do to track them down. In the meantime, we start to dig. Talk to the employees of the facility, talk to the neighbours and friends of the Franks. They've not long moved to the area – they moved

21

here because of Frank's new job at the lab. As you also know, we've got Stuart here, who's about to become a protestor himself."

Kate saw Stuart draw himself up a little, putting his shoulders back. Anderton gestured to him. "Stuart, take it away. Give us the details of your assignment – those you can disclose."

Stuart waited until the room was completely silent, a smile that Kate interpreted as smug on his face. Look at him, revelling in the attention, she thought. Cocky so-and-so.

"Hello everyone," Stuart finally said. "Welcome back, Kate."

He flashed her a smile which she limply returned. Why was he welcoming her back as if he ran the place, when he didn't even know her?

"As most of you know, I'll soon be going undercover with the protest groups and activists who are currently targeting MedGen," Stuart continued. "I'll be there for a minimum of one month, reporting back regularly to see if we can uncover any evidence on the bombing. You may or may not know this, but in this type of situation, there's a distinct hierarchy to the groups, different... layers, shall we say." He spread his hands to demonstrate. "You've got the bottom rung; the mostly respectable protestors, the Guardian-readers, the lefties. Not normally much to worry about there, unless you're scared of petitions and badly made placards."

There were a few grins at this. Kate gritted her teeth.

Stuart went on. "As you get further up, in amongst the more... *serious* protestors — the more militant ones – that's where you start to get useful info. That's where you have to dig in deep, get yourself accepted, before people start opening up to you." He hesitated, looked as though he was about to say more, then clearly thought better of it. "Anyway, as I said, I'll be working in the field for a month, probably longer." He looked over at Anderton.

"Right, thanks, Stuart," Anderton said immediately. "Stuart will be reporting back regularly to myself. And, of course, if any of you run up against him in the course of the enquiry, you are on no account to acknowledge him as one of us. Naturally. I would hope that I wouldn't even have to say that."

"You didn't have to," said Olbeck, with a smile.

Anderton nodded. "Well, exactly. Right, now we're a bit more up to speed, we can get on. Mark, why don't you and Kate head to MedGen and continue the interviews there? Theo, you and Jane continue with the neighbours and friends of the Franks. Rav, you're on desk duty today, I'm afraid – I need someone manning the office. Anyone got any questions?" No one had. "Right, let's get on. Kate – come and see me in my office in five minutes' time?"

There was the usual sense, once Anderton had

left the room, that a great mass of energy had suddenly dissipated. The team slowly returned to their work.

"Come and grab me after your meeting with Anderton and we'll head off," Olbeck said to Kate. He gave her a cheery wave and made his way down to the end of the office.

Kate watched him go. She was keenly aware that Stuart was watching her closely and she wouldn't give him the satisfaction of knowing she was upset. She blinked, bent her head studiously to the papers on her desk and pretended to read them. This was awful. She'd been looking forward to getting back to work for so long, and now she was here, she couldn't help but think longingly of her home; the sofa where she'd spent so many hours, the garden where she'd sat in the sun and breathed deeply and got better. She mentally counted down the seconds until five minutes had passed, casually pushed back her chair and made her way to Anderton's office.

"Come in," said the familiar voice at her knock. As she pushed open the door, Kate thought of all the times she'd stepped through this doorway into the office, remembering all the emotions that she'd experienced in this room. She took a deep breath and set her face to neutral.

Anderton waved towards a seat. "Shut the door behind you," he suggested and Kate did so. As she turned to take her seat, Kate remembered the last time she'd been in here with a closed door and what had happened. She wondered whether he did, too. Would that ever happen again or was he always going to be the one that got away? For a moment, she felt horribly bleak. Why was she even thinking that? What was wrong with her?

"So," said Anderton, flinging himself in the seat opposite her, his desk between them. "How's your first day back going?"

"Fine," said Kate, totally unwilling to let him know how hard she was finding it. "I'm easing myself back into the swing of things."

"That's good," said Anderton, hunting for something in one of the desk drawers. "Take it easy, though. No need to rush anything."

"No," said Kate. Was he trying to tell her something? She shifted a little in her chair and almost unconsciously, her hand went to the small of her back, feeling for the ridge of her knife scar.

"It's hard coming back after a long time away," Anderton continued. "Believe me, I know. But you get there, in the end. In a couple of weeks' time it'll feel like you've never been away."

"I'm sure you're right," Kate said. When was he going to stop with the platitudes and actually say something meaningful?

A silence fell. Kate cast about desperately for something to say, suddenly convinced that Anderton was doing the same. Their gaze met and there was

25

a long, charged moment where the air hung heavy with everything that was not being said.

"Well," said Anderton eventually, looking down at his desk. "I won't keep you much longer."

"No," Kate said.

"I'm sure you've got lots to catch up on."

"Yes," Kate said.

"Let me know if you need any help with anything."

Kate sighed inwardly. "Yes," she said again, standing and pulling her hand back from where it was rubbing at the scar.

"Thanks, Kate. And seriously—" Anderton finally stopped fidgeting with his desk drawers and looked at her properly. "It's good to have you back."

"Is it?" asked Kate, unable to hide a smile. Anderton said nothing in response but winked. Kate left the office, struggling to keep her smile from becoming a wide grin.

Chapter Two

As she and Olbeck drove away in his car, Kate began to feel better than she had all day. Sitting across from her partner – former partner, she reminded herself – she could feel herself relaxing back into familiarity. This was how it used to be; the two of them driving from interview to interview, case to case, talking about the crime and the suspects and what they were going to do next. It was easy, it was comfortable; like putting on a pair of well-worn-in shoes. She had been worried that Olbeck would now treat her like a subordinate, someone to be talked down to and patronised, but of course he didn't. He treated her as normal. She felt a little ashamed that she'd even entertained the thought. You're getting paranoid, she chided herself.

"Did Anderton brief you?" asked Olbeck.

Kate shook her head. "Nope. Not a sausage."

Olbeck gave her a puzzled glance. "That's odd. I thought that was why he—" He didn't finish the sentence and Kate could hear him mentally shrugging. "Anyway, want me to run through things with you?"

"Please. I feel like I'm totally floundering at the moment."

"No problem." Olbeck shifted gears and settled back in his car seat. "Right, basically, the MedGen Facility is the brain child of two research boffins, Jack Dorsey and Alexander Hargreaves. They met at university – one doing chemistry or something like that, one doing something a bit less scientific. Dorsey's the boffin, Hargreaves is the businessman, as far as I can see."

"What is it that they research?"

"Oh, God, something totally esoteric, I don't understand a single bit of it; it's something to do with human metabolism – something like that. Anyway, the end result is that their original research got them into developing new methods of weight loss pills. That's partly why all these protestors are up in arms – all this animal suffering for something as frivolous as the diet industry. Something like that, anyway."

"Right."

"Made them both huge amounts of money. But we'll find out a bit more when we interview them. When I spoke to them before, it was just to check alibis and get first impressions, we didn't get a chance to go into the nitty-gritty of the business."

As he spoke, Olbeck flicked on the indicator. The

car turned off into a smaller road that continued for about half a mile before ending in a formidable gate. The gate that blocked the road was topped with razor-wire and the glassed-in booth by the entrance had an impregnable look. Olbeck drew the car into the side of the road and approached the guard, sat impassively behind the screen. After a long and suspicious perusal of their warrant cards, he pressed the button that drew back the gate and they were able to drive through.

"They're obviously expecting trouble here," said Kate, noting the cameras and the high fences that surrounded the site. "They clearly value security. Why wasn't Michael Frank more careful?"

Olbeck shrugged. "He was new to the job. He was in a hurry. And, security or no security, they've never had a car bombing before. No one was expecting *that*."

"I suppose so," said Kate. She watched as the buildings of MedGen came into view. They looked as if they had once been some kind of government building, perhaps ex-council offices or something similar, but had clearly undergone a huge and expensive renovation.

Olbeck parked the car at the front of the main building. The two officers made their way through the automatic glass doors, into a reception area that wouldn't have looked out of place in a luxury spa. Behind the curving steel and glass of the front desk sat a polished young woman in a tight black suit. Her well-shaped eyebrows twitched upward minutely as Kate and Olbeck flashed their warrant cards but otherwise she preserved the neutral expression of a shop window mannequin.

Another glossy young woman, equally stone-faced, came out to usher them through to what was clearly the inner sanctum of the executive offices. Kate looked around as they waited. The glass-topped coffee table before them was scattered with a variety of glossy magazines and broadsheet newspapers; The Times, The Spectator, Tatler, Racing Times. The fittings were plush and expensive, with several vaguely medically themed objects d'art dotted about the room. An abstract painting on the wall, full of swirling reds and blues caught her eye. As she got up to take a closer look at the tiny label at the bottom of the frame, she realised it was actually a hugely magnified photograph of a cell from the smaller human intestine.

"Nice," she murmured to herself as the glass door to the office opened.

Both directors of the company emerged to greet them. Jack Dorsey was a man who missed being handsome by a mere whisker; he was just a shade too thin, his face a little too bony for true good looks. He, according to Olbeck's notes, was forty six – he looked older, partly because of his receding sandy-grey hair and the deep-cut wrinkles at the corners of his eyes. But there was still an element of freshness in his general demeanour; something of youth and vigour and keenness. Kate could imagine he was devoted to his job.

His partner, Alex Hargreaves, seemed to embody the opposite qualities. Attractive, in a kind of coarse, slightly overfed way, Hargreaves was very much the businessman; well dressed in a Jermyn Street suit, thick black hair combed back, and the hint of a jowl developing above the collar of his expensive linen shirt.

When they were all seated in Alex Hargreaves' huge office, with coffee cups placed before them by the black-suited automaton who had shown them in, a small silence fell. Jack Dorsey sat forward in his leather chair, his bright blue eyes fixed on Olbeck's face. Alex Hargreaves lounged back in his seat, one leg crossed over the other.

Olbeck began by thanking them for their time. He was almost always courteous to begin with, Kate remembered.

"We're following up a number of leads in relation to the murder of Michael Frank," Olbeck continued. "What would be really helpful for us is to find out more about the victim himself. Can you tell us anything about him? What was he like?"

Both men went to answer, glanced at each other and half-laughed. Dorsey inclined his head in a kind of 'after you' gesture and Hargreaves nodded, leaning forward in his chair. "I interviewed Michael for the role – well, we both did, but I took the first interview. We're always on the lookout for new talent here, the brightest and the best. Michael was pretty well established in his old firm, but he was looking for more responsibility, something a bit more challenging."

Olbeck nodded encouragingly.

"Anyway," Hargreaves went on. "He got the job. He was far and away the best candidate, hands down."

"What was he like?" asked Kate, thinking she should speak, finally.

"Like?" Hargreaves looked confused.

"Yes. What did you think of him? Personally, as opposed to professionally, I mean."

"Well... I—" Hargreaves looked a little confused. "He was a nice bloke, I suppose. Bit quiet."

"He *was* quiet," broke in Dorsey. The others in the room looked at him and he went on, unruffled. "He was quiet but he wasn't shy. He had one of those personalities that grow on you. He had... character, I suppose you would say. To use an old-fashioned term."

Hargreaves looked at his partner with an expression that Kate couldn't quite place. It was half admiration, half something else. Impatience? Irritation?

"I see," said Olbeck, nodding. "Was Mr Frank

well-liked in the company? Did he mix well, make friends?"

The two directors looked at one another. Hargreaves almost, but not quite, shrugged.

"I don't know," Dorsey said, after a moment. "I certainly don't think he was *dis*liked. Unfortunately, he wasn't here long enough for me really to be able to make a judgement on his popularity, poor man."

"Did you have a lot of contact with him, day to day? Both of you, I mean?"

Hargreaves nodded. "A fair amount. We had weekly meetings of the exec team – the executive team, I mean – and Michael was part of that. Ad-hoc meetings during the week, as and when were needed. Budget meetings once a month. Is that the sort of thing you mean?"

Olbeck nodded. "It all helps to build a picture. We'll need to speak to any of the staff who worked closely with him, who reported to him, worked under him, you get the picture. Would you be able to take us down to where he worked?"

Dorsey clasped and then unclasped his hands. "We can, Inspector. It's—" He hesitated for a moment and glanced across at Hargreaves. "These are the areas of... well, animal experimentation. If you get distressed by that sort of thing..."

Kate refrained from pointing out that they were here to investigate the brutal murder of a human being. She waited for Olbeck to answer and, when he didn't, said crisply "I'm sure we'll take it in our stride, sir."

"There's very little *actual* experimentation here," Hargreaves said quickly. "But that's what the media and the protestors are all over, of course."

"That's something else we'll need to talk to you about," Olbeck said. "I see you've got fairly good security on site but what with the bombing, this is clearly not enough. Is there someone we could talk to about that, as well?"

Dorsey nodded. "I'll ask our Head of Security to come up now. He'll be able to take you through the set up here, and you'll be able to ask any questions that you want."

"Fine," said Olbeck.

They were shown back into another plush meeting room, with a crystal carafe of water and two glasses placed before them on the table by the receptionist, who barely nodded in response to Kate's thanks. Olbeck's phone buzzed.

"Damn it," he said, checking it. "I need to head back after this meeting. Anderton wants me on a conference call."

"Oh?" said Kate. She was conscious of a spurt of something that felt suspiciously close to jealousy. Why did Anderton want Olbeck on a call and not her?

Because he's a DI, Kate. And you're not. She

clamped down on the thought, telling herself it didn't matter.

"What about interviewing his co-workers?" she asked. "Want me to do that?"

"No, that can wait until tomorrow. You and Theo can come down and work them together. Okay?"

"Okay," muttered Kate. She didn't actually agree – wasn't time of the essence? – but she wasn't ready to start querying Olbeck's orders. Not quite yet.

There was a knock on the door and a tall, bald man walked in, introducing himself as Terry Champion, Head of Security. Thickset and muscular, with one of those protruding bellies which makes the owner look eight months pregnant, Champion was nevertheless helpful and forthcoming. Ex-army, Kate surmised. She wondered why it was that security guards and chiefs were always bald? She went off into a mini-reverie whilst Olbeck asked the questions, fantasising that an excess of testosterone was responsible for both their choice of occupation and their hair loss, before bringing herself back to reality with a start.

"Oh yes, lots of threats, tons really," Champion was saying breezily. "We X-ray all the post as a matter of course."

"Any letter bombs or anything like that? Suspicious packages?"

Champion rubbed his chin. "Nothing that bad,

to be fair. Occasional package of dog shit, but we take that in our stride."

"Not very pleasant," Kate said, feeling she should contribute something.

Champion looked at her with an expression she couldn't decipher. "No," he agreed. "But better dog shit than a car bomb, eh?"

"Not much you can say to that," Kate said to Olbeck, as they drove back to the office. He chuckled.

"I need to brush back up on my interviewing skills, I think," she continued gloomily.

"You're just out of practice. You'll get the hang of it again."

"I know."

"It's your first day back, woman. Take it easy."

Kate sat on her hand to stop it reaching around to her back. "I know," she said, again.

Olbeck glanced over at her and then patted her on the knee. "Chin up," he said, and Kate tried to smile.

Kate was just shutting down her computer, feeling more tired than she had in months, when her mobile rang. Andrew's name flashed from the screen. As always, there was a quick flash of something, a feeling she couldn't quite pin down and didn't exactly want to. Was it anticipation?

Annoyance? No, that was too strong. It wasn't comfortable, though, and Kate didn't like that. She didn't want to think about her visceral reaction to her first sight of Anderton today and how different it was to the reaction she had to her boyfriend calling her.

She answered the phone.

"How's the first day back going?"

As soon as she heard his voice, Kate felt better. She relaxed back into her chair. "I'm surviving. That's about all I can say."

"You must be buggered."

"I am."

"That's a shame." He hesitated for a moment. "I was hoping to take you out to dinner. But if you're really tired..."

Kate considered. She was hungry and she knew Andrew would pay – he insisted on it. But he also had a penchant for fine dining and very formal restaurants, with white linen tablecloths and attentive waiter service, and Kate just didn't have the energy for it today.

"Why don't you come over to mine?" she suggested. "We'll get a takeaway and chill out on the sofa."

"Really?" He sounded eager and, for a moment, she felt a flash of irritation. This time, it was easy to interpret. Just as quickly, she felt guilty. What was wrong with her?

"Definitely," she said, making her tone extra warm. "I'd like to see you."

Kate switched her computer off, stood up and pulled her coat on. She had the sudden absurd impulse to walk around everyone's desks, saying goodbye to each person individually. Of course, she wouldn't do that but... it was still too strange, too new for her to be able to just walk out, throwing a casual 'goodnight' over her shoulder. She wondered how she was going to get home. Olbeck was out, Theo had already left and she hadn't driven herself. Bus it was, then, or should she treat herself to a taxi, just this once?

Outside the station, as she stood vacillating from one choice to the other, a horn pipped and a second later, Andrew drew up in his BMW. She felt a welcome burst of pleasure at seeing him and climbed into the cool interior of the car, smiling broadly. Her greeting kiss was heartfelt.

"Well, you look better than I thought you would," said Andrew, brushing her hair back from her cheek. "Not quite as knackered as I was expecting."

"It's all a front," said Kate, strapping herself in. She let her head fall back against the headrest and sighed, closing her eyes. "Now I can relax."

"You certainly can. Sure you want to go home?"

Kate nodded fervently.

"Right you are, my sweetheart."

The traffic was heavy and it took them longer

than normal to get back to Kate's house. When he was able to, Andrew rested a hand on Kate's thigh and she tried not to show the irritation that caused her. Then she felt guilty for feeling that. Why shouldn't he rest his hand on his girlfriend's leg? I'm just tired, she told herself. I don't want to be pawed about. Then she felt guilty again, even for thinking the words. She put her own hand on his leg and gave an answering squeeze and he turned his head and smiled at her.

It was Kate who unlocked the door of her house – she hadn't yet given Andrew a key. He'd offered to get her one for his place but she'd declined, knowing that she would then have to make a reciprocal offer. She wasn't ready for that, yet. Stepping inside the hallway, she was enveloped by the sense of pleasure that her house always induced in her; the calm, tidy, ordered interior that greeted her every day, the furniture and pictures and ornaments that she'd chosen with care and attention.

"Shall I cook?" asked Andrew, throwing his jacket over the newel post of the staircase.

Kate set her teeth for a moment and hung it on the hooks by the front door. She shook her head. "Don't bother. Let's get a takeaway."

Kate placed her shoes neatly in the shoe rack and put her hands to the small of her back, stretching. Her scar throbbed.

"No, don't worry about that," said Andrew. "I'll cook. I'd like to."

"Suit yourself," said Kate. She pulled herself up, realising how ungrateful she sounded. "That would be lovely. Thank you."

Andrew tipped her a salute and headed to the kitchen.

Kate made her way upstairs.

"I'm going to jump in the shower," she called. She prayed Andrew wouldn't want to join her. At that very moment, she wanted to be by herself again; just her, in her cosy house with the door locked and her phone switched off, licking her wounds and trying to see a positive way forward. Andrew, nice as he was, was a distraction. Kate rubbed her face, pulling her fingers over her closed eyes. She couldn't remember being this tired in a long time. Perhaps I'm not up to it anymore, she thought, and felt a cold thrill of fear. If she didn't have her work, what did she have?

Andrew called up to her to tell her he was making her a cup of tea and, this time, she felt grateful he was here.

Kate closed the bathroom door behind her, hesitated, and then locked it. So what if Andrew tried to come in? He'd have to learn that she needed her privacy, sometimes. There was nothing wrong with wanting to take a shower on your own, for God's sake. Kate came to with a start, realising she was arguing with a fantasy version of Andrew inside her head again. The real Andrew was downstairs in the kitchen, singing untunefully along to the radio. Kate rubbed her face. She was starting to think she should have turned his offer of company down tonight, made up a little white lie. But no – she did want the company, didn't she?

The shower was throwing clouds of white steam into the air. Kate dropped her clothes neatly into the hamper and climbed under the spray of hot water. Immediately she began to feel better. The sense of defeatedness, of hopelessness, that had surrounded her ever since she'd sat down at her new desk at the station, began to disperse. She poured a generous dollop of expensive shower gel into the palm of her hand, sniffing the perfume appreciatively. It would work out. She would be fine. She would slot back into her work as if she'd never been away. Her fingers went automatically to the ridge of the scar, sliding over it. The shower gel fell to the floor of the bath with a splat and Kate tutted with annoyance and yanked her hand away from her back. Just *leave* it, Kate. Think about something else, for a change.

Showered and dried, dressed in her slobbing-at-home clothes. Kate paused at the entrance to the kitchen. Andrew was clattering pots around, chopping herbs, whistling as he worked. Kate watched him for a moment, unobserved. He's good looking, he's smart, he works hard and he cooks, she thought to herself. You're lucky to have him. She smiled, but at the same time was suddenly aware of how tired she was. She leant her head against the door frame, closing her eyes.

"Whoah," Andrew's voice said and Kate felt his big arms close around her shoulders. She leant forward, resting her head against him without opening her eyes. "You're just about dead on your feet, aren't you?"

Kate nodded, too tired to even speak.

"Well," said Andrew. "My considered medical opinion is you should go straight to bed. Come on—" He lifted her bodily and she gave a tired giggle. His physical bulk was one of the most attractive things about him; when she was in his arms, she felt safe, enfolded, protected. Andrew carried her up to the bedroom and deposited her on the bed. Kate rolled gratefully under the covers.

"Shame," said Andrew softly, stroking her hair back from her forehead. "I was hoping for a little bit more than that. But hey, there's always first thing tomorrow, right?"

Kate grinned tiredly at him. Then she muttered something like 'thanks', pulled the duvet cover up to her nose and was instantly asleep.

Chapter Three

KATE WAS WOKEN THE NEXT morning by the shrill electronic peal of her phone, buzzing and skittering over the bedside table like a large black insect. She grabbed for it blearily, whilst behind her Andrew groaned and rolled over. It was Theo.

"Pick you up in an hour, right?"

"What?"

Theo sounded incredibly alert and wide-awake. Kate rubbed her eyes, looked at the clock. Seven ten am.

"What bloody time do you call this?"

"The early bird catches the worm, Kate. Rise and shine! I'll pick you up in an hour. See you then."

The bleep of a disconnected signal sounded in Kate's ear. She sat up, rubbing her eyes again.

"I've got to go," she said to Andrew, who was half buried beneath a pillow. He was working normal hours this week, which meant a nice, nine-thirty start. He grunted something.

Kate got ready, guiltily relieved that she had

seemed to have got out of having sex with her boyfriend. That was the last thing she felt like, first thing in the morning, especially after an exhausting day before. She planted a kiss on Andrew's cheek, bristly with morning stubble, grabbed her bag and made her way downstairs.

Theo was dressed in another nice suit. It looked expensive and he looked altogether older, and to be taken seriously. Kate caught sight of herself in the passenger seat mirror. She really must get her hair cut. How old was the jacket she was wearing? Five years? She shifted a little in her seat and her scar began to throb. Surreptitiously, she tried to rub it.

"You all right?" asked Theo. "You look knackered."

Kate grimaced. "Gee, thanks. It's my second day back on the job, I'm amazed I'm even awake and coherent." She ran her hands through her hair, shook her head, made an effort. "Where are we going?"

"Back to the lab. Mark wants us to interview the co-workers, this time."

"Oh yes," said Kate, a little dazedly. "I remember."

"You and Mark spoke to the directors yesterday, right?"

"That's right. Jack Dorsey and Alexander Hargreaves."

"What are they like?"

Kate rubbed her face. "We'll speak to them again and you can see for yourself."

Again, they were shown into the plush waiting room. Theo whistled under his breath and paced around a little. Kate subsided into an armchair and fought the urge to put her head against the back of it and go to sleep.

Theo picked up the copy of the Racing Times and flicked through it.

"Didn't know you were a betting man," murmured Kate, as much for something to say as anything.

"Well, I'm not, really," said Theo. "Flutter on the National, that's about it. Few quid on the gee-gees, now and then. Nothing amazing."

Alexander Hargreaves opened the door to the waiting room himself. Kate saw his gaze go to the magazine in Theo's hand and the minutest flicker of some kind of emotion crossed his face, gone almost before she could register it. Then he was striding forward, his hand outstretched. "Sorry to keep you waiting, DS Redman. How can we help you today?"

Kate introduced Theo and asked whether they could have a chat with Michael Frank's colleagues. "Are you able to take us there, Mr Hargreaves?"

Jack Dorsey entered the room. Again, Kate was struck by the energy he brought with him, a sort of compressed vividness that he carried about.

After the pleasantries, Kate repeated her question.

"I'm free for the next half an hour," said Jack Dorsey. "I'm happy to take you down there."

"Great," said Theo, cutting across Kate who was just opening her mouth to reply. She smiled to hide her annoyance. "Thanks for meeting with us, Mr Hargreaves."

Alexander Hargreaves shook both their hands. His palm was smooth and warm against Kate's, the press of a large signet ring on one finger almost making her wince as his fingers closed around hers.

"Any help we can give you, any at all," he said, his tone serious. "Michael was a great scientist and he had children too... whatever we can do to help."

Jack Dorsey led them both along a series of corridors, down two flights of stairs, through numerous security doors and finally brought them to a halt in front of a glass panelled door, again with a security system fitted to it. Behind his shoulder, through the glass panel, Kate could see several people in white coats bent over microscopes and making notes on clipboards.

Jack Dorsey's manner changed a little. Up in the office suite, he'd been serious and calm, although still with that air of suppressed energy. Here, clearly his natural environment, it was as if that energy became apparent. His eyes noticeably brightened.

"This is the lab," he said, tapping in a code on

the security panel of the door. They heard the *thunk* of a heavy-duty lock drawing back. Dorsey held the door open for them.

Kate was first struck by the warmth... and the smell. Underneath the antiseptic wash of disinfectant was the earthy, musty smell of mice. She could see a bank of stacked plastic cages over by the far wall. The two people who'd been visible through the door looked up curiously as the detectives and Dorsey approached.

"These are Michael's colleagues," Dorsey said. "Sarah Brennan and Parvinder Goram." He introduced the detectives and the two scientists turned looks of mixed comprehension and apprehension towards them.

Kate opened her mouth to ask a question but just as she was framing the sentence, Theo got there first.

"You worked closely with Michael Frank?" he asked, directing the question to Sarah Brennan as the older of the two women. She was in her late forties, with smooth dark hair and a pleasant, careworn face.

She nodded. She looked at Jack Dorsey with an expression Kate couldn't quite place.

"Don't worry, Sarah," Dorsey said smiling. "It's all perfectly straightforward. I'll leave you with the detectives."

The laboratory door *thunked* shut behind him.

Kate raised her eyebrows in what she hoped was a pleasantly interrogative way. "You worked closely with Michael?" she asked Sarah Brennan again.

"Yes." Sarah tucked her hair behind her ears. She was wearing a rather lovely pair of diamond earrings. "The project he'd been hired for was something I'd been interested in for a while. I transferred over from another department when I heard he'd be working here."

Again, Kate began to say something and Theo cut across her. She hoped her annoyance didn't show on her face.

"You knew him well, then?"

Sarah nodded again. Kate's eyes dropped to her hands, noting the lack of a wedding ring, the short, blunt, practical nails.

"We'd worked together before he came here, actually," Sarah was saying. "We were both at the same lab back in Northumberland - this was back in the nineties. Quite funny that we ended up working together again, but not that surprising. His research background was in a quite a niche area and mine is the same. I suppose it was fairly inevitable that we would end up working together again."

"How about you, Doctor Goram?" Kate jumped in before Theo could draw a breath. Again, she was forcibly reminded of how different working life was going to be now. She and Olbeck had interviewed together seamlessly, years of knowing when to talk and when to keep quiet meaning they didn't even have to think about who was going to lead on the questions. Theo's style was obviously very different.

Parvinder Goram was probably younger than thirty-five. She had a thin, pretty face and eyes that were ringed with shadow that could have been exhaustion, but might have been genetic. Just glimpsed underneath the collar of her lab coat was a bright red fluffy jumper, which struck an oddly frivolous note.

She was less forthcoming than Sarah Brennan, or perhaps she had less to say. "Michael was my supervisor," she said. "I'm two years into my doctorate. So, technically, I'm a 'Ms', not a doctor, yet."

"Sorry," said Kate. "How was Michael to work for?"

Parvinder cast a glance at Sarah, a glance that was too quick for Kate to decipher. "He was fine," she said.

"Can you tell us anything more about him?" said Theo. He edged forward a little, his shoulder nudging Kate's, as if he were literally trying to budge her out of the conversation. She gave him an annoyed glance.

Parvinder took in Theo's handsome face and well-cut suit and her manner changed. She smiled a little flirtatiously. "He was a bit of a cliché, in some ways," she said, with something that was almost a giggle. Sarah Brennan's face flickered a little. Parvinder went on. "I mean, he was quite absent minded and he was always late for everything. He was always losing things. I can't remember how many times he'd shout out from his office, 'has anyone seen my... whatever,' and mostly we hadn't."

"He was very good at his job," broke in Sarah. She shot a look at Parvinder that Kate interpreted as repressive. "Yes, he was a little absent minded, now and again, but that's because he was always thinking about something more important than the minutia of daily life."

"I see," said Kate. "Well, I—"

"Can you tell me anything about Michael's personal relationships?" Theo cut across her again.

Kate couldn't help glancing at him in surprise. Where was he going with this?

"What do you mean?" asked Parvinder.

"His relationship with his wife, his friends," said Theo. "Did he have a good relationship with his wife, that you know of?"

Sarah Brennan was frowning. Parvinder looked mystified. "I suppose so," she said, "I don't really know."

"Where were you going with that?" asked Kate as they drove back to the office.

"What d'you mean?"

"The questions about Michael Frank's wife. What was all that about?"

Theo gave her a strange look; half indulgent, half annoyed. "Get with the program, Kate," he said. "We're assuming that this is a straight act of terrorism. Aren't we?"

Kate nodded, reluctantly.

"Well," said Theo, changing gears with a cocky flick of his wrist, "What if it's not? What if it's for some other reason? A personal reason?"

"A *car bomb*?" Kate tried to keep the scepticism from her voice. "What the f—" She cleared her throat and tried again. "I mean, what the hell are you talking about?"

"It's just an idea," said Theo, airily. "I'm just running with it. What if it's not a terrorist attack at all? Perhaps his wife wanted him dead. Perhaps he's pissed another scientist off. I don't know, I'm just thinking out loud."

"Right," said Kate. "His respectable, middle-class wife and mother of his two children decides to forego the divorce court by planting an explosive device under his car. Yes. I can see how that might happen."

Theo reddened a little.

"I'm not saying it's *likely*. I'm thinking aloud, here."

Kate made a mammoth effort to stop herself casting her eyes up to the ceiling.

"Have you told Anderton your theories?"

Theo changed down gears as they approached a T-junction, this time with more of an annoyed shove. "No, I haven't. I don't have any *theories*. I'm just thinking aloud."

"All righty, then," said Kate, this time not bothering to keep the contempt from her voice.

"Feel free to chip in with any ideas of your own," Theo said snappily. She heard him mutter the rest of the sentence under his breath and despite pretending not to hear, heard the words clearly enough. *If you have any, that is.* She breathed in sharply through her nose, clamped her mouth shut, and looked out of the window. They spent the rest of the return journey in silence.

Chapter Four

KATE WAS GETTING USED TO these early morning wake-up calls. This time it was Olbeck, calling to tell her he was *en route* to pick her up.

"Sorry about the late notice. Tried calling you last night, but I couldn't get through."

That was because Kate had crawled straight to bed after getting home the night before, not stopping to wash, eat or check her phone. She decided not to mention that.

"Sorry," she said, sitting up in bed. "I didn't check my phone."

"No worries. Anyway, we're interviewing Mary Frank this morning and I need you along. Pick you up in an hour, okay?"

Polton Winter was a tiny village, saved only from being a hamlet by the presence of the ancient village church. The gateway of the Franks' house was visible from the churchyard – at least what was left of it. The stone wall that encircled the garden at the front of the house was nothing more than a pile of rubble and the young beech tree that had stood by the driveway was stripped of all of its branches on one side. Sap had run like blood down its blackened trunk.

The house itself was a small, pretty, Georgian cottage, built of what had once been golden Bath stone. The windows had already been replaced, but the front of the house was chipped and pocked with tiny pieces of metal, which had embedded themselves in the porous stone.

Olbeck parked on the driveway. As Kate got out of the car she felt herself shiver as she realised they had parked on the blackened piece of tarmac where Michael Frank's car had stood.

The two Frank children were at school. Mary Frank opened the door to the two officers and Kate was immediately struck by her haggard face and shaking hands. She managed a flicker of a smile – convention was obviously too strong for her not to be able to show some form of greeting – but as she led them through to the living room, she hunched her shoulders as if expecting a blow to fall upon her.

The two officers took seats. Mary Frank remained standing for a moment, clasping both arms across her body. "Could I get you tea – coffee?" she asked, faintly.

"No, nothing for me," Kate said immediately and Olbeck also murmured his polite refusal.

Mary Frank sat down rather too suddenly in an

armchair. Kate eyed her uneasily. The woman was like a spring wound tight, every muscle clenched. A nervous system flooded with adrenaline. Post-traumatic stress disorder, was the phrase that sprang immediately to mind and Kate knew all about that.

Olbeck was very gentle with Mary, speaking softly and calmly. "I know this must be very distressing for you, Mrs Frank, but I was wondering if you could just take us through the few days preceding the – the incident." Mary Frank's shoulders jerked and she tried to cover the movement but shifting in her chair and re-crossing her legs. Olbeck continued. "It would be really helpful if you could tell us anything about anything strange you might have noticed. Any strangers. Anything slightly odd, perhaps."

Clearly, they had already had a preliminary interview with Mary Franks and this was a follow up. Kate sighed inwardly. She was coming at this case so behind it was difficult to know whether she was missing anything important.

Mary Franks was looking blindly down at the arm of her chair. The fingers of one hand pulled compulsively at the thumb of the other, over and over again. "I don't think so," she said in a low voice, after a moment's silence. "I can't remember anything. It was – it was just normal."

"Try and cast your mind back to the day before. What did you do?"

Mary Frank closed her eyes for a moment. Kate thought she was probably running through the memories in her head, watching the pictorial record of her life scroll past – the last moments of the life she'd known before it was blown to smithereens by eight pounds of plastic explosive.

"I don't remember, exactly," she said, in a quiet voice. "I was at work in the morning – I teach adults with learning disabilities, part time – but I came home for lunch. I did some housework, I think. I can't remember exactly, I'm sorry—"

"Not to worry," Olbeck said soothingly. "You didn't notice anyone hanging about the house or driveway? No strangers came to the door?"

"No. No, I don't think so."

"Did Michael mention anything to you that seemed significant, in the light of what happened?"

Mary's mouth cramped. She shook her head mutely.

Olbeck glanced over at Kate. She knew he was thinking what she was thinking: that this interview was pointless. Mary Frank was too traumatised, too broken to even think about what she was saying. She didn't want to remember anything about the days leading up to the bombing because she then had to accept that it happened, and she wasn't ready to do that yet – not by a long shot.

"Right," said Olbeck after a moment. "I can see

that this is still very painful for you, Mrs Frank. Have Victim Support been in touch with you?"

"Hmm?" Mary Frank was staring at the floor, her fingers pulling compulsively at a fold of her jumper. "What's that?"

"Have you been offered any counselling by Victim Support?"

After a moment, the woman's blank stare focused a little. "Oh, yes," she said faintly. "They've been very kind. Everyone has been very kind."

Olbeck exchanged a glance with Kate. She shifted forward in her chair, preparing to get up.

"Wait," said Mary Frank suddenly. She was frowning slightly, her foggy gaze clearing. "There was something – it's probably nothing..."

"What was it?" Kate asked, trying not to sound too eager.

"It was one night, about a week before the – before it happened. Michael and I were just going to bed and he said 'that car's been parked out the front for ten minutes now. Do you think they're lost?'"

"You didn't recognise the car, then?"

Mary Frank shook her head. "It was dark and there's only one streetlight near the house. It was quite a big car. A dark colour, dark blue, perhaps?"

"Can you remember the make of car?" asked Olbeck.

Mary Frank frowned again, biting her lip. She was silent for a moment. "I'm sorry, I can't remember anything more about it," she burst out. Tears shone in her eyes. "Do you really think it might – might have had something to do with – with—"

"I can't say, Mrs Frank, I'm sorry. We'll have a look at the local CCTV for that night. What night was it, can you remember exactly?"

This time Mary shut her eyes. She clenched her hands together, pressing her fingers against one another until the knuckles went white. "It was the Tuesday... that's right... the Tuesday before it happened. Michael was late coming to bed because he'd had a call from his brother that went on for a while. They don't speak often." She tripped herself up over the tense she'd used and gulped. "I mean, they *didn't* speak often, so when Paul rings, they chat for a long time. That's right, I looked at the clock when Michael came up and it was past eleven o'clock. He twitched the bedroom window curtain as he walked past it and that's when he mentioned the car. I had a quick look but I couldn't see much. Whoever it was drove off just after I looked out of the window."

Kate was scribbling quickly in her notebook. She didn't imagine there were many cameras in Polton Winter, if any, but it would be worth a try to see if anything had been picked up.

"Thank you, Mrs Frank," Olbeck said, putting a great deal of warmth into his voice. "That's really helpful. If you can remember anything else that might help, you will let us know, won't you?"

Mary Frank nodded fervently. She looked better than she had at any point since they arrived, but still, even as they said goodbye on the doorstep, Kate didn't want to leave her. She made a point of mentioning Victim Support again as they took their leave and made sure Mary had her business card.

"Poor woman," she said to Olbeck as they drove away.

"Yes, indeed."

They were both silent for a moment. Kate watched the sun-dappled beech woods roll past the windows of the car. She remembered Mary Frank's compulsive pulling of her thumbs as she sat in her chair and realised her own hand was creeping towards her back, almost stealthily. She put it back in her lap with an exclamation of annoyance and Olbeck looked over, surprised, but didn't say anything.

STUART WALKED BEHIND THE GROUP of protestors, far enough back so that they wouldn't realise he was there, close enough to get a good look at them. They were heading for one of few the pubs in the area that would serve them; Stuart had seen a handwritten sign on the door of one of the other nearby pubs that had said 'No Protestors'. He was determined that this would be the opening he was looking for.

The pub was a dive – sticky carpet, yellowed wallpaper, stench of old cigarettes embedded in the fabric of the seats. Stuart waited until the small group of protestors had been served, got his own pint and sat down unobtrusively in a corner, ostensibly reading the tabloid newspaper that had conveniently been left at the table, but really taking a closer look at the people he was tailing. He was looking for the weak spot, the one who would let him in.

There were two women and three men in the group. Stuart focused on the women – it was almost always easier to strike up a conversation with a woman. The two he was watching were both young, both quite pretty under the crazy dyed hair and facial piercings and crappy clothes. Which one? He chose the smaller, slighter one, the one who laughed a lot, looking up at the men in the group with a face that was slightly too eager.

Stuart waited until the girl of his choice made her way to the loo. He waited until she re-emerged and, seemingly on his way to the bar again, gently bumped into her.

"Oh, sorry!" she said in a surprised tone, even though it was technically his fault and that was when he knew he'd picked the right one.

Her name was Rosie and she was twenty-two, having just graduated from some no-mark university. Stuart bought her a drink, gave her his best cheeky-chappy grin and made sure she got a good look at his Plane Stupid T-shirt.

"Were you at the Heathrow protest?" she asked, gesturing to his chest.

"For sure. Were you?"

She shook her head. "Not that one. We went along to the camp, though. That was where I met James, actually."

Stuart followed her gaze to one of the other protestors; a rangy, tall, dark-haired guy who was casting curious glances back at them. Rosie waved him over and introduced Stuart.

"This is Mike," she said. Stuart inclined his head slightly and held out his hand. After a moment of hesitation almost too brief to notice – although Stuart did notice, that's what he was trained to do – James shook it.

"All right?"

"Yeah. Rosie was just telling me all about how you guys met." Stuart had stepped back a little, out of Rosie's personal space. Good decision, as the next moment had James sliding an arm around her waist and pulling her closer to him.

"You an activist, then, man?" James asked, with just the slightest hint of hostility in his voice.

Stuart knew how to counter that. Find the commonality, find the shared experience –

something that will soften someone towards you. There was always something. With James, it was his accent. Stuart had spent some time in Newcastle and he could hear the faint intonation of someone who'd once lived there – for how long, he couldn't tell – but it was there, in James's voice. That was his opening.

"You know, man, I think I've met you before," Stuart said, getting a nice mix of doubt and delight into his tone. "Did you go to Newcastle?"

The faint suspicion clouding James face cleared. "Yeah. Yeah, I did. Did you?"

Stuart improvised a quick story about visiting a mate at the university and hitting some of the student bars there. He mentioned a few names – "John, John Richards, you know him? No?" and when James came up with the names of several other Johns who'd been students there, Stuart was able to feign recognition and claim a vague acquaintance with one of them. This, coupled with a few anecdotes centred around some riotous drinking at the campus bar, was all that it took. A few pints later and James was his new best friend, Rosie shunted off to the side and almost forgotten.

"You coming to the protest tomorrow?" James asked as they said goodbye at the end of the evening. Stuart was as sober as a judge, being a master in the art of seemingly drinking without actually doing so.

The other activists were nine tenths drunk, falling against one another, laughing.

"For sure," said Stuart. "That's why I'm here, man."

"Cool. See ya, then. Oh, and there's a party tomorrow night, as well."

"Even better," said Stuart, grinning. He winked at Rosie, bumped his fist against James' and, raising a hand to the others, set off for the grim little bedsit he was renting for the duration of this job.

Chapter Five

ANDREW'S HOUSE HAD A VERY pleasant conservatory at the back of the kitchen, where one could sit drinking good coffee from a fine white china mug, toes snuggled into slippers, looking out at the pretty garden and distant hills beyond the back fence. Kate drew her dressing gown more snugly about herself and sipped her hot drink, watching the sparkle of the morning sunshine on the lawn, bejewelled with a million little beads of water.

Andrew was busy in the kitchen and the delectable smell of frying bacon soon filled the room. Kate smiled to herself. Here she was, dressed in a fluffy white dressing gown, with her good coffee and her feet up on the bar under the table. The Sunday papers were scattered over the tabletop. She could almost imagine herself to be in a glossy photo-shoot of a lifestyle magazine. How did someone like me end up here? She remembered chaotic mornings in her mother's filthy kitchen; the shouting, the hunt for a clean bowl, the rancid smell of the milk that hadn't been put away in the fridge overnight. Too many children, too much stuff everywhere. Trying to get herself ready for school, trying to find a shirt that wasn't too dirty. Kate shuddered and looked about her again, at the cleanliness and luxury, taking comfort in the beautiful view through the sparkling windows.

A hand appeared from behind her, bearing a plate loaded with food.

"Dig in," said Andrew. "If you manage to get through that lot, I'll be amazed."

"I'll give it my best shot," said Kate, smiling up at him. "Wouldn't want you slaving over a hot stove for nothing."

Andrew sank into a chair opposite her with his own full plate in front of him. He picked up the sports section of The Times, flapped it open and settled back in his chair with a loud sigh of contentment. Kate began attacking her breakfast with appreciative noises.

Andrew looked up after a moment. "I like seeing you at my breakfast table," he commented.

"I like being here. Particularly when I get a full English breakfast cooked for me."

Andrew smiled. "Perhaps we ought to make it a more permanent arrangement," he said, flipping the page of the newspaper.

Kate froze, laden fork halfway to her mouth. A

piece of bacon fell back onto her plate. "Sorry?" she asked, after a second that felt more like a minute.

"Make it a more permanent arrangement," repeated Andrew. He was still perusing the newspaper and his tone was casual. "What do you think?"

Kate put her fork back down on her plate. "Well—" she began carefully, but was interrupted when her mobile rang, loud and insistently. She could feel it vibrating in her dressing gown pocket.

She fished it out. The shock of Andrew's words was nothing compared to the shock of seeing Anderton's name glowing on the screen of her telephone. She fumbled to answer it.

"Hello, sir."

She could tell something had happened even before he spoke. There was something heavy in the dead air humming between the satellite signals that brought his voice to hers.

"Kate. Sorry to interrupt whatever it is you're doing. I know you're not supposed to be working."

"It's fine," Kate said quickly. She could feel her pulse quicken. "What is it?"

"The usual. Worse than usual. I need you here right away."

"No problem—"

"I'm sending Mark over to get you. He can fill you in on the way."

"No problem," said Kate again. She felt a little

winded. Worse than usual...what the hell did that mean? Then she remembered Anderton didn't know she wasn't at her own home. She explained.

"Stanton's place? Yes of course – Mark said something—" Anderton sounded... well, she couldn't quite put her finger on it. Pissed off? Amused? It was the merest trace of something, gone in an instant as he went straight back into professional mode. "I'll tell Mark to take a detour then. Does he know where your paramour lives?"

"Yes he does." *I've been seeing him for almost a year, you know.* "I'll be ready."

"Right. See you soon."

"Do we have an ID on the victim yet?" asked Kate quickly, before he could ring off.

Anderton was silent for a moment. "We've ID'd one of them," he said, eventually.

"*One* of them?" repeated Kate and Andrew looked up from his paper at her tone.

"This is a multiple murder, Kate. Didn't I say?" *No, you didn't.* "It's one of the co-directors of the MedGen Facility."

"Alex Hargreaves?" asked Kate, shocked.

"No, Jack Dorsey." Dead air hummed down the line again for a second. "That's all we've got at the moment. See you soon."

The broken line bleeped in Kate's ear. She put the phone back in her pocket. Andrew was looking at her from across the table, his mouth crimped.

"Was that work?" he asked. She knew he knew it had been.

"Yes. I've got to go."

"Oh, not today, surely?"

Kate tried to look sorry. "I have to. I'm really sorry, Andrew. You know what it's like."

Andrew looked down at the paper again and flipped another page with an irritated flick of his fingers. "Yes, I know what it's like," he said, quietly. "Oh well. If you have to, you have to."

"I'm sorry," said Kate, more sincerely this time. She quickly got up and gave him a kiss. "I'll let you know how I get on."

"Fine."

She kissed him again and then turned and made for the stairs and the bedroom, racing for her clothes and feeling that welcome sense of anticipation, tinged with a little fear, that she always felt at the start of a new case.

Within ten minutes, she heard the beep of Olbeck's horn outside. She grabbed her bag, kissed Andrew again as he sat, still in something of a sulk, at the breakfast table and left the house, shutting the door behind her firmly. She flung herself into the passenger seat rather breathlessly.

"Fill me in. Please, fill me in."

"Alright, alright. Keep your hair on." Olbeck reversed the car out of the driveway as Kate buckled herself in. "We've got plenty of time."

"I heard it's Jack Dorsey."

"You heard correctly. Dorsey, a currently unidentified male, and Dorsey's wife."

"Jesus." Kate was silent for a moment, looking ahead unseeingly through the windscreen. "What are the first ideas? A domestic? Or something else?"

"I don't know and can't speculate. I haven't even been to the scene yet. It's in Poltney Carver; village on the far side of Abbeyford."

"I know it. Well, vaguely. Isn't it the next village to Poltney Winter? Where Michael Frank lived?"

Olbeck nodded crisply. "That's right."

"Hmm," said Kate. "Well, I guess we'll know more when we get there."

It was a beautiful spring day: the kind of day where the British countryside looks its best. Its best is very good indeed, thought Kate, looking out of the car window. The trees were newly clothed in leaves of a bright fresh green and the sky was a clear, dazzling blue. Faint white wisps of cloud lay on the horizon. The hedgerows and fields were dotted with a profusion of colourful wildflowers, like dainty embroidery on a smooth, green blanket.

The car passed the sign for Poltney Carver. It was a small but clearly affluent place: the driveways of the pretty cottages that lined the few streets of the village housing large, expensive cars. Several of the houses of golden stone sported window boxes, filled with golden, dancing daffodils and the smooth upright heads of pink and white tulips. Ahead, Kate could see a police car and a couple of uniformed officers guarding the gateway to what was obviously Jack Dorsey's house. Olbeck slowed the car to flash his identification and they were waved through.

The drive was a long one, winding through sun-dappled woods where the first early bluebells could be seen in a faint, bluish haze under the beech trees. Olbeck slowed a little as they approached the next blind bend in the driveway. It was as well that that he did, because the second they rounded the bend, Kate yelled and Olbeck gasped as the broad white snout of an ambulance filled the windscreen of the car from side to side. The siren screamed as Olbeck yanked desperately at the steering wheel. The two vehicles passed each other with a sliver of space between them. Then the ambulance was past, blue lights flickering briefly over the interior of the car. Hedgerow twigs and leaves thrashed at the windows as the car juddered down the rough edges of the road, before burying its bonnet half in and half out of a hazel hedge. The engine stalled.

Kate and Olbeck remained motionless for a moment, Kate gripping the sides of her seat with both hands. As she realised they'd come to a stop and she was still in one piece, she released her grip, finger by rigid finger, and slowly sat back in the seat.

"Jesus, that was close," she said, when she could be sure of her voice.

Olbeck had gone pale. "You're not wrong. What a brilliant piece of irony that would have been; killed by a speeding ambulance..."

He fumbled his seatbelt open with shaking hands and got out of the car, holding onto the door like an old man. He groaned. "God, would you look at my paintwork."

Kate got up out of the car herself. She was feeling sick with the backwash of adrenaline, although the fresh air helped. "It's a mess," she agreed. "Still, could have been worse."

Olbeck was bent over the bonnet, tutting and flicking at the myriad scratches. "I've probably buggered the suspension as well," he muttered. "God Almighty..."

He swung himself back into the driver's seat and gingerly tried the key in the ignition. The engine turned over a few times, then sputtered back into life. "Move back a bit, Kate, while I try and get this out."

Kate moved back obediently. Olbeck nudged the car back out of the hedge and onto the open road again. He revved the engine a little. "Seems to be okay. Let's get on."

Kate hopped back in, feeling more normal. The same thought struck the two of them simultaneously and they turned to one another in the same instance.

"The ambulance—"

"Blue lights—"

"That means – that must mean—"

"One of them is still alive," said Olbeck. "Probably. Let's go find out, shall we?"

He drove very cautiously along the rest of the winding driveway, sounding his horn at every corner. They encountered no other vehicles. The driveway ended in a wide sweep of gravel in the front of a beautiful, four storied house of the gothic Victorian type, built in Bath stone with a multitude of glittering mullioned windows and a small fountain playing in the smooth green circle of lawn in front of house. There were several cars parked already and two uniformed officers guarding the half-open front door.

After the shock of the near-accident, Kate hadn't anticipated what they would soon be seeing at the crime scene. The beauty of the surroundings somehow made the fear of what was to come worse. She felt a twinge of pain in her back, deep within the scar. As Olbeck turned off the engine, she took a deep, shaky breath and unclipped her seat belt.

Chapter Six

THE SILENCE WAS THE FIRST thing that she noticed.
The only noises she could hear were natural ones:
birdsong, the rustle of leaves, the musical tinkle of
the falling water in the fountain. Their footsteps
sounded abnormally loud as she and Olbeck
crunched across the gravel to the front door. Kate
took another sweeping look around before they
entered the house. There was a security camera
mounted up on the front wall of the building,
another trained on the step on which she stood.
Alongside a car that she recognised as Anderton's,
and two patrol cars, there was a large black four
wheel drive vehicle, something that looked like a
classic vintage sports car and another silver four
wheel drive. Did those belong to Jack Dorsey and
his family? Kate looked again at the front of the
house, with its myriad windows. Behind the nearest
window to the front door, she could see thick folds
of expensive fabric held back by a glossy curtain
tie. Against the wall of the house were flowerbeds

planted with old-fashioned, cottage garden flowers: hollyhocks, larkspur, well-clipped rose bushes. There was money here – a lot of money.

Olbeck and Kate slipped on gloves and boots and stepped forward into a small inner hallway, wooden panelled and unfurnished except for a delicate little wooden table stood against the far wall. On its surface, a mercury glass vase held an arrangement of spring flowers. As she walked forward, Kate caught a faint breath of their delicate scent, obliterated a moment later by the heavy, metallic tang of blood. It should have been a warning but she still had to look twice as they walked out into the larger, inner hallway. The walls were painted a warm cream and the overhead lights were on. Kate thought for a moment that the hallway was tiled with glossy, wine-coloured tiles, a decorating choice that contrasted rather oddly with the rest of the interior. The illusion lasted a second, until she realised that the floor tiles were actually a conventional black and white, in a checkerboard pattern. They looked a glossy scarlet because they were submerged in a flood – a veritable lake – of blood.

A body lay in the middle of the red pool that filled the hallway from edge to edge. The body of a middle-aged man, tall and heavy, dressed in a dark tracksuit. His hair was cut brutally short and the bald spot at his crown shone under the overhead lights. He was waxen-white, the cleanly incised wound in his neck just visible.

The police officers regarded him in silence. Kate could feel her face freezing to a neutral expression automatically. It was partly a learned response – you realised early on not to show any sign of distress or emotion if you didn't want the piss ripped out of you by the male officers – but it was partly a defense mechanism, as well. Keep your face blank and somehow the horror of what you saw was reduced, just slightly. Just enough to cope.

"Is all the blood his?" Kate asked Olbeck, in a subdued monotone.

He was standing at the edge of the blood, staring intently at the body. Kate realised there was no way to get past the blood pool to the other side, without walking through it. Not a chance. Scene of Crime would kill them if they attempted it – she could already see two white suited technicians giving them uneasy glances from further down the hallway.

"Looks like it," said Olbeck. He raised a hand to the SOCOs to placate them. "We'll go round, guys. Don't worry."

They retraced their steps back through the first little antechamber and stepped back into the sunshine. Kate lifted her face to the warmth of the rays. The air felt incredibly fresh after the tainted stuffiness of the hallway. She closed her eyes briefly. The redness of the sunshine through her closed lids recalled the bloody lake inside, the body of the man spread-eagled within it, as if swimming.

They walked around the outside of the house, looking for a side entrance. Through a wrought iron gate in a box hedge, the path opened out onto smoothly manicured lawns, with a white iron conservatory before them. There were more cameras here, trained on the French doors that led into the conservatory. The doors stood open and the edge of a green curtain, made of what looked like heavy, lined silk, could be seen flapping gently in the breeze.

"Look at all these cameras," Kate said, gesturing. "Surely we'll have something from one of them?"

"Let's hope so." Olbeck had caught sight of Anderton and Theo, standing on the threshold of the house. At the same moment, their colleagues noticed them and lifted their hands in greeting. Theo looked as if he'd got up too early after a heavy session the night before. Anderton looked fairly normal, perhaps just a trifle pale.

"Good morning," he said, as Kate and Olbeck approached. Kate didn't smile in response – it felt inappropriate in the circumstances. "I suppose you've been through the front?"

"Tried to," answered Kate. "Couldn't get past the body."

"That's the security guard. His name's Darryl, not sure on the surname, yet."

"Not much of a guard, was he?" Olbeck said, a remark that from him that was quite remarkable in its unexpected callousness. Kate raised her eyebrows. Perhaps he was more unnerved than he was letting on.

"What else have we got?" she asked.

Instead of answering, Anderton gestured towards the house. "Go on through. You'll soon see. Come back out and tell me what you think."

"You're not coming?"

Anderton gestured again. "Just go and get your first impressions," he said.

Theo sat down rather abruptly on a convenient garden bench and lit a cigarette. His hands were shaking slightly. Kate was going to say something, tease him a little about coming to work on a hangover, before deciding that she'd better keep her mouth shut. She and Olbeck exchanged a look and then stepped through the doorway, into the conservatory.

The same heavy green silk curtains they had glimpsed from the garden had been drawn over the panes of glass that made up the walls. The floor was tiled in the same checkerboard pattern as the hallway. Kate and Olbeck stepped cautiously through into the house. They came out into a large room; a sitting room, beautifully furnished, with pale green walls, a polished dark-wood floor and a large, cream rug. Antiques stood against the walls, too many beautiful things to take in at once. The lights were on, blazing from the overhead chandelier and the curtains were drawn back from the ceiling height windows.

The beauty of the room made what was in it worse. Jack Dorsey's body lay in front of the fireplace. Kate had to look twice to be sure it was him, he had been so savagely attacked. She looked once at the knife wounds to his face and chest and then looked away, swallowing. She groped for her neutral mask and tried to fix it back onto her face, which wanted to grimace and crumple. She could feel Olbeck at her side, his arm touching hers, and the warmth of his body momentarily brought a little comfort. She fixed her eyes on the rug, purposefully not looking at the body. Dorsey's blood had spurted in arcs and splashes and sprays, marking the pale rug in an awful abstract artwork. It was dry now, brownish red, stiffening the long fibres of the carpet. She realized now why Theo had looked so bludgeoned. Her gaze was drawn to another dark splash on the far wall, next to the huge, gilt-framed mirror that reflected the horror contained within the four surrounding walls. Something written in blood, in dragging, jagged letters a foot high. KILLER.

She and Olbeck remained at the edge of the room while the technicians did their work. Camera flashes went off at monotonous intervals, Kate trying not to flinch at every one. After what felt like an hour, but was probably only ten minutes, Olbeck turned to Kate and, with mutual appeal in their glance, they turned and left the room.

Once again, out in the open air, Kate drew in a shaky breath. The air outside tasted indescribably fresh and sweet after the abattoir inside. She and Olbeck walked over to where Anderton and Theo sat on their bench. Anderton looked up in silent enquiry.

"Jesus," Olbeck said eloquently. He sat down on a low garden wall that edged what looked like a kitchen garden.

"Exactly," agreed Anderton. "Butchered. I think that's the word I'd use."

"Was there another victim?" asked Kate, remembering the ambulance.

"Dorsey's wife, Madeline. She was lying next to him when we got here. Terribly injured but, incredibly, still alive."

"Alive?" asked Kate. She felt her pulse quicken. "Do you think she'll make it?"

"I don't know. I hope so. But – well, if you'd seen her..."

"What were her injuries?"

"Knife wounds, same as Dorsey. She looked like she'd lost a lot of blood."

"God," said Olbeck. He pushed himself up off the wall and began pacing around. "Was it – I mean, we're certain there was an intruder?"

Anderton looked pleased. "Ah, you're thinking it could be a domestic? It's possible, although from the fact that the security guard is also dead, unlikely. We'll obviously know more if Mrs Dorsey pulls through."

"Who reported it?" asked Kate.

Theo spoke up for the first time. "Cleaner," he said, a little thickly. Clearing his throat, he threw his cigarette butt into a flowerbed and went on. "She's currently in the kitchen with a WPC, having hysterics."

"Understandably," Anderton said, also getting to his feet.

Kate remembered something; a flashback from her interview with Jack Dorsey at MedGen. His desk, a silver-framed photograph: blonde wife, blonde children, arms interlinked. She felt a coldness spreading in the pit of her stomach. "The children," she said, feeling as if she didn't quite have control of her mouth. "The Dorsey children... are they – has anyone checked—"

Anderton looked at her properly for the first time since she'd arrived. A flicker of sympathy crossed his face. "They're at boarding school, both of them. Both safe. Thank fuck," he added, almost as an afterthought.

Kate sat down on the wall herself, feeling almost queasy from the wave of relief that spread over her. Then she thought about having to break the news

to them. Sorry, kids, about your mum and dad...
Resolutely, she turned her mind away from the
thought.

"We've searched the rest of the house and
we're spreading out into the grounds." Anderton
had been speaking for a few moments before she
became aware of what he was saying. She tried to
concentrate. Anderton went on. "There's no sign
of forced entry. We haven't yet had a look at the
CCTV footage, that's obviously top priority once
the SOCOs are finished here."

He stopped speaking and for a moment, they
all faced each other, sharing an odd moment of
solidarity. Kate, despite all the horror of the scene,
felt a warm thrill of belonging, of coming home,
back where she should be. It was the first time she'd
felt it since she had come back to work and, for a
moment, she luxuriated in the sensation. It was as
if life had suddenly come back into focus.

"So," said Anderton quietly. "Thoughts?"

"Someone came to the door," said Kate. "The
security guard let them in and he was walking back
through the hallway when they attacked him."

"Given the position of the body, I'd say that was
a fairly accurate guess," Anderton said. "And why
would he let someone in through the door, given
that he's supposed to be guarding the house?"

"Because it was someone he recognized," said

Kate. "Someone he knew. Someone he didn't think was a threat."

"Exactly. Hopefully the CCTV will tell us exactly who that was."

"Is that likely?" asked Olbeck, in a cynical tone.

"Well, we won't know until we look. I agree, anyone who comes ready to kill three people is probably going to take some pains to conceal their identity." He raised a hand to his head, tousling his hair in a characteristic gesture. "You mentioned a possible domestic, Mark. I don't think we should discount that, out of hand. I don't think we can comfortably do that. We don't know enough about the victims, their relationship with each other – we know nothing about the Dorseys' marriage, their history. I agree with you, Kate, that this has all the hallmarks of an outsider, an intruder killing – all I'm asking is that we need to keep an open mind."

Everyone nodded.

Theo lit another cigarette. "The writing on the wall," he said. "What's with that?"

"Yes," agreed Anderton. "The literal writing on the wall. What's that telling us?"

"The most obvious answer is that it's a message, isn't it?" suggested Olbeck. "Telling us Jack Dorsey's a killer. It's a motive."

"Is it?" asked Anderton. "Perhaps it's a very mentally disturbed person, telling the world what he – or she – has done. It's a sign. 'I am a killer'."

Olbeck shrugged. "Yes, could be."

Kate rubbed her temples. "We don't yet know who the intended victim is, do we, sir?" she asked. "I mean, if there was *one* intended victim. I'm assuming it's Jack Dorsey – and maybe his wife..."

"That's a reasonable assumption," said Anderton. "But nothing is definite."

"It's just – the guard looked like – well, like that was a quick, almost clinical killing. To get him out of the way, perhaps. Whereas Jack Dorsey..." The image of his body flashed up in Kate's mind's eye and her voice faltered for a moment. "That was savage. That was *anger*."

Chapter Seven

KATE HAD HAD A CLEAR picture of the cleaner in her head, especially after she learned her name was Mary Smith. Middle-aged, working class, overweight and homely – Kate chastised herself for the stereotype, but somehow, the mental picture persisted. It was something of a shock to find that Mary Smith was in her very early twenties, blonde, slim and with an impeccable accent. She was dressed casually, in a pink T-shirt and tight blue jeans, with her long hair pulled back into a low pony tail. Her good looks were apparent at a second glance, but at first sight were subsumed beneath the utter shock and terror distorting her face. Mary's pink T-shirt had a jarring pattern of red dots and jagged stripes, which Kate realised, after a moment, were blood stains.

The officers sat down. The WPC, Mandy – Kate knew her very vaguely – kept a comforting hand on Mary's trembling shoulder and handed her another mug of tea. Enough sugar in it to make the spoon stand up straight, Kate had no doubt. She had a sudden vivid flash of her grandmother saying exactly that, as an eight-year-old Kate handed her an afternoon cuppa. What was Nana's other tea-related phrase? Strong enough to trot a mouse on. Kate blinked and dismissed the memory, bringing herself back to the present and the interview at hand.

"Now, Miss Smith," began Anderton. "I'd like to thank you for talking to us. I appreciate what a dreadful shock this must all have been."

Mary Smith said nothing but her shuddering increased. A little tea splashed over the edge of the mug clamped in her hands. Mandy bent over and gently removed it, keeping her hand on Mary's shoulder.

"I'd just like to hear what happened when you arrived at the house," said Anderton. "Can you take us through what happened?"

Mary Smith had been holding herself rigid. At Anderton's gentle request, she gave a small nod and winced, as if that tiny movement hurt her. "It all looked totally normal from the outside," she said after a moment, in a tone so low she was almost whispering.

"You have a key?" Anderton asked, after it became clear that she wasn't going to say any more.

Mary swallowed and made a visible effort to pull herself together. "Yes, I've got keys to the front door and the alarm codes. I got here – I think it was about ten thirty, normal time. It all looked so normal."

"And then what happened?" Anderton prompted.

Mary swallowed again. "I unlocked the front door—"

"Wait," Olbeck interrupted. "The front door was locked?"

Mary nodded. "That's why I didn't realise – I didn't think anything was wrong... it would normally be locked."

"Right. Sorry – go on."

Mary pinched either side of her nose, shutting her eyes momentarily. "I unlocked the door and went into the hallway and I saw – I saw Darryl—"

She drew in her breath in a great sobbing gasp. For a moment, Kate was sure she would collapse again, but after a moment she went on, her voice shaking.

"The lights were off and it was dark – it's always quite dark in there, as there aren't any outside windows, so I put on the light and – Darryl was there, *dead*, in all that blood... I thought – I thought I was dreaming for a moment. It was like... like something from a nightmare. I stepped in the blood, I didn't even realise I had – I was frozen for a moment—"

Her voice failed and she drew in another whooping breath. Mandy patted her arm encouragingly.

"Go on, Miss Smith," said Anderton.

"I ran towards him, I – I could see he was dead, logically I could see he was dead, but I couldn't help it – I was going to feel his pulse but then I saw the cut in his neck and I couldn't touch him—" She looked pleadingly at the officers, as if they would take her to task for it. "I'm sorry but I couldn't, I was hysterical – I didn't know what to do..."

"You're doing really well, Miss Smith – Mary. What happened then?"

Another shuddering breath. Mary's eyes were closed, her chest rising and falling fast. "I was going to go on, go through the house to see if Jack and Madeline were there – I thought – well, I wasn't really thinking anything, I just was kind of blindly going forward – and then I thought 'suppose whoever did this is still here,' and that was it... I just ran, ran out the house and down the driveway. I – I don't remember much else."

As Anderton told them later, a woman from the village, walking her dog along the main road, had seen Mary come screaming out of the driveway, blood-streaked and hysterical, and caught her in her arms. She was the witness who'd called the emergency services.

"So, let me just check that we've got everything," Anderton said, very soothingly. "You arrived, as normal, at about ten o'clock this morning. You unlocked the door, which is what you would normally do, and you walked in and found Darryl on the floor."

Mary nodded.

"Would Jack Dorsey and his wife normally be at home during the day on a Friday?"

Mary took in another deep, shaky breath. "Jack definitely wouldn't be. He's always at work. Madeline's sometimes in, but just as often she's out. That's why I had the key and the codes."

"I see. How did you get the job here?"

Mary looked confused for a moment before her face cleared. "Through the university. I'm a student at Bath Spa."

"How long have you been working here, Mary?"

"Um... not long. About six months."

"That's great. Could I just ask you to hold on one moment? I'm sure Mandy will make you another cup of tea."

Anderton drew his officers to one side for a moment. "Theo, can you take over here? I don't think there's much more she can tell us, other than what she's already said, but you never know. Kate, Mark, can you get on and see if you can find the CCTV? Quick as you can."

They all nodded. Theo sat back down next to Mary. Olbeck inclined his head towards Kate. "After you."

"No, I insist," said Kate, standing back. "After you, DI Olbeck."

"Just get on with it," said Anderton, half smiling. "I'm off."

"Where are you off to, sir?" Kate asked as they let the kitchen.

Anderton's face became grim again. "Hospital," he said, briefly. "To see if Madeline Dorsey's alive or dead."

Chapter Eight

"SO WHERE'S THIS PARTY, THEN?" Stuart asked as he helped the others dismantle the table and load it into the back of the dirty white van that they'd parked just outside the gates of MedGen. Stuart, along with James and Rosie, had been manning the leaflet table since he arrived at ten thirty that morning. The leaflets had a variety of gruesome pictures displayed beneath shouting black headlines. Stuart had seen several people, obviously out walking their dogs, stop, looking interested in what they were doing, catch sight of the pictures of bunnies clamped to tables and puppies punctured with needles, and recoil, walking on with a nervous glance back. He wondered whether to point out that these leaflets seemed to be totally counterproductive to their cause and decided not to.

"We're heading there now. Want a lift?" asked Rosie. She was struggling to lift a heavy box into the back of the van. Stuart lifted it from her arms and slotted it into place. "Oh, thanks. Why don't you come with us?"

"Sure, will do. It's not like I even know who's throwing it," said Stuart. "Whose house is it?"

Rosie had turned away to gather more boxes. James was already climbing into the front seat of the van. Seeing he wasn't going to get an answer, Stuart shrugged and went to help Rosie collect the last of the boxes. He wasn't dressed for a party, but what the hell – he doubted very much it would be a black-tie affair.

They drove for about twenty minutes, Stuart crouched uncomfortably in the back of the rattling, clanking van, with boxes of leaflets sliding into him as they drove around corners. He wiped some of the dirt off the back window to see if he could see where they were going. James was following the dual carriageway out of the town, heading for the outskirts on the north side, where the village of Armford had long been swallowed up by the creeping boundaries of Abbeyford. Stuart pushed a box away from him and noted the road sign that flashed past. They were driving into a housing estate built around the nineteen thirties, by the look of the houses, travelling along progressively narrower roads until they drew into a cul-de-sac where the gardens of the houses backed onto a scrubby piece of woodland. The van stopped with a jerk. Stuart opened the back doors and clambered out, wincing at the bruises on his thighs inflicted by the sliding boxes.

It was about six o'clock, not yet quite dark. They had parked outside a run-down detached house, the front garden paved with concrete. Stuart followed James through the open door of the house and was immediately met by a wall of heat and a fug of cigarette and spliff smoke so thick it felt like a physical barrier. Trying not to inhale, he followed James's denim-clad back through to what turned out to be the kitchen, although Stuart was fucked if he would dare eat anything produced in the fetid little room. There wasn't any food anyway, merely a sink full of beer and a table crowded with wine bottles and cans. People were everywhere; smoking, talking, shouting, waving to one another. Most were young, most were clearly activists – there were a lot of piercings and tattoos and interesting hairstyles. Stuart had tied his dreadlocks back this evening. One thing he was looking forward to, after this assignment finished, was getting the whole bloody lot cut off. That would be first on his list of things to do once he was back in the real world.

He, James and Rosie grabbed beers and made their way out through the crowds to the garden beyond the kitchen door. It was just a square of lawn and a tumbledown fence, but the evening air was beautiful; soft and warm in a way that English spring nights so rarely were. There was an outside light which, despite the dingy shade, had attracted a fluttering cloud of moths and insects forming a moving corona.

"Whose house is this?" asked Stuart.

"Dunno who it *belongs* to," said James, "But we know a few of the guys who live here. It's a squat."

Stuart should have guessed. He thought longingly for a second of his own flat back in London; minimal furniture, many gadgets. "Who's that, then?"

Rosie was crouched awkwardly on a low brick wall that ran partway along the length of the garden boundary, rolling a joint. She gave the papers a final, expert twist.

"Angie lives here, doesn't she?" she asked, of no one in particular. "And Rizzo. I don't know really, people just seem to drift in and out. I stayed here for a bit myself, when I first came down."

"Before you met me," said James.

"Right."

She lit the joint, took a deep drag and handed it to Stuart. He lifted it to his lips. As he could spend the evening seemingly doing some serious drinking while actually remaining as sober as a teetotal judge, he could also do a credible impression of a man toking hard without actually doing so. The Bill Clinton Method, he thought, with an inner grin.

Quickly as he decently could, he passed the joint on to James. He needed to know more about the loosely knit group he'd infiltrated, and this party was the perfect opportunity to do some tentative preparatory digging. He'd tried, subtly, to find out a little more about James and Rosie's immediate friends and fellow activists but, for people single minded about a certain cause, they were frustratingly vague about their colleagues and mates. Perhaps here at this party, he could start to ascertain his next move, who he should be taking a deeper interest in.

He went back inside to fetch more beers, an exercise designed to continue the good impression he was making on James and Rosie and to give him the opportunity to stake out a few of the fellow partygoers.

He walked slowly; it was impossible to do otherwise, given the crowded space, but he wanted to keep his ears open to the possibility of overhearing something interesting. He reached the kitchen. For a moment, the press of bodies in front of him opened up a little and that was when he saw her.

She was standing under the harsh strip light, bathed in a strident white light that would have been utterly unforgiving to nine out of ten women. She was the tenth. The brilliant white light turned her face to a beautiful blank mask, bleaching out all the little imperfections that you saw in normal skin. Her hair was jet black and very short, almost a sculpted cap that hugged the contours of her perfectly shaped head. All Stuart could see for a moment was a sulky red mouth and two huge dark eyes, as her gaze met his. A challenging stare. For a second, he was aware of a surge of anger, almost as strong as the opposing one of desire.

The challenging, almost aggressive look was gone in the blink of an eye. Stuart wondered whether he'd imagined it. Now she was looking over at him with the tiniest trace of a smile, her face softened and open. He made up his mind.

"Hi."

She looked up at him from under her long lashes. "Hello."

"I'm Mike."

"Hi Mike. I'm Angie."

His ears pricked up a little at that. "This is your gaff, isn't it?"

She nodded. Up close, he could see faint freckles on her pale skin, the merest dusting of them, like gold glitter spread over her little nose. She wore a slash of black eyeliner and that red lipstick, but no other make-up.

"It doesn't belong to us. We're squatting here. It was empty and unloved so – we took it on."

Stuart looked around at the squalid room surrounding them. Angie followed his gaze and laughed. The laugh transformed her face, from beautiful but chilly sculpture to a more appealing, boyish gamine. Stuart could feel the faint warmth of her body from a few inches away, they were standing so close.

"Yeah, I know," she said. "It's pretty shitty. But beggars can't be choosers."

She had an unexpectedly deep voice for such a delicate looking girl, rather husky, as if she were just getting over a bad cold. She confirmed the reason why after a moment of silence between them. "Coming for a smoke?"

"Lead on," said Stuart, who sighed inwardly at the thought of another fake toking session. Still, if that was what it took...

They passed James and Rosie on their way through the garden and Angie stopped when she saw them. She and Rosie greeted one another with a kiss on the lips, which inwardly raised Stuart's eyebrows. James didn't seem to mind, looking on with a slightly lecherous smile. The four of them stood and smoked and talked. Stuart tried to quell his impatience. He wanted to talk to Angie on her own.

"Who's 'we'?" he asked Angie, in a break in conversation.

She looked at him with those large dark eyes, eyelids made heavy with dope. "What?"

"You said 'we' took it on. The house."

"Oh, yes," she said. She passed the joint to Rosie and hoisted herself onto the brick wall, kicking her heels against the bricks. "There's a few of us here. Rizzo and Charlie, mostly. People come and go."

"Seen Kitten lately?" asked James.

Stuart had his eyes fixed on Angie's face and he saw the tiny ripple of some kind of emotion go over her face, gone in an instant. She pushed her hair back from her forehead.

"Not lately," she said, a trifle coolly.

There was a moment's silence. Then Rosie started talking about the protest, how she was sure it was having an effect, *they must be getting pissed off with us by now...* Stuart kept his eyes on Angie. The mask had come back down over her face and, after a moment, she slid off the wall.

"Getting a drink," she said. She gave Stuart a look he couldn't quite decipher and after a moment, she walked away.

Stuart hesitated. He wanted to follow Angie and he wanted to know more about this Kitten.... He made up his mind in a split second, no time to dither and walked off after Angie, miming a 'getting a beer' motion to James and Rosie. He heard Rosie's derisive snort behind him and took a moment to wink at her before quickening his pace to keep Angie in view.

She walked straight past the table of drinks in the kitchen, through to the hallway and turned up the stairs. He saw people, men mostly, turning to stare at her as she passed. He followed her up the stairs, looking at the smooth white skin at the nape of her neck where her hair grew in twin dark points. There was a second, smaller staircase on the landing and Angie climbed that, Stuart following her. The stairs ended in a blue-painted door at the top and beyond the door was what was obviously Angie's bedroom.

Stuart paused for a moment in the doorway, getting his bearings. It was difficult because, as he quickly realised, the walls and ceiling were covered in tiny, glittering shards of mirror glass, hundreds of them; a mosaic of reflections, lit only by the candles that stood in the tiny iron heath in the chimney breast. Stuart turned slowly, watching an infinite number of tiny Stuarts turn with him, moving in the mirror pieces. There was hardly any furniture in the room, just a small chest of drawers, a bookcase stuffed with books and a double mattress on the floor, covered with a patchwork quilt. There was a large amount of computer equipment arranged on a desk against the wall, the oversized screen dominating the room. Several video cameras were arranged neatly next to the keyboard. Angie sat cross-legged on the quilt, a small wooden box in her lap, watching him with a small, amused smile.

"Far out," said Stuart. He put a finger out to the nearest wall, feeling the individual edges of the mirror pieces. "How long did it take to do?"

"About ten years," said Angie absently, occupied

in a hunt for something within the wooden box. "No, not really. About three weeks. I was almost blind by the end of it, fiddling with all those tiny little pieces."

"Amazing." Stuart realised what she'd been hunting for as she withdrew it from the box – a small plastic bag half filled with white powder. She looked up and saw him watching.

"Want some?"

Stuart didn't hesitate. "If you can spare it."

"Wouldn't have offered if I couldn't'." Angie patted the mattress beside her and Stuart sat down carefully.

He watched as she shaped the powder into two lines, neat snowy drifts on the top of a CD case. Even after years in the field, he still felt that tremor of anxiety at the thought that he, a police officer, was about to do something illegal. He would still do it, of course, as small a line as he could. The last thing he needed now was to arouse Angie's suspicion.

She offered him the CD case and he shook his head. "Ladies first."

She grinned and ducked her head and while she was still head down and rubbing her nose, he took the case, whisked the majority of one line off of the surface with his thumb and quickly inhaled the miniscule amount that was left.

He was hoping that the coke would make Angie open up a little, but when she turned to him with glittering eyes and parted lips, he could see that she had a more wordless activity in mind. He had a second of hesitation, training too strong in him to be able to ditch it without a qualm, but then her lips were on his and her hands on him, and all his thoughts of ethics and morals were swept away in an instant of reckless abandonment.

Chapter Nine

KATE AND OLBECK BEGAN A preliminary check of the building. The house was beautiful, but the horror of what had happened within it somehow tainted its elegance and charm. Kate, climbing the main staircase, was reminded of too many horror films where the victim climbed unknowingly to their doom. The heavy silk and velvet drapes that hung at every window seemed to bulge unpleasantly, as if concealing someone within their folds, waiting to jump out. The rooms and hallways seemed full of too many shadows, even with the bright sunlight outside. She shook herself mentally and told herself not to be so stupid, but ridiculously, she found herself hurrying to stay close to Olbeck as they moved from room to room.

"Anderton said it's been searched already, right?" she asked, as they entered what was obviously the master bedroom. It had a four poster bed within it, draped in white linen. The covers were bunched messily at the foot of the bed.

Olbeck nodded absently, as he surveyed the room. An empty mug stood on one of the bedside tables, beside a stack of books. Kate went over to see what they were. No fiction at all; a pile of learned scientific works and what looked like several PHD theses. Kate checked her gloves were intact and picked one up, flicked to the front page, read a few paragraphs in increasing confusion and put it down again.

"See, that looks like English but it can't be, because I can't understand one word of it."

Olbeck grinned. "Well, he's a boffin, isn't he? Dorsey, I mean."

"Was," corrected Kate.

The grin fell from Olbeck's face. "Yes. Was." He walked over to the matching bedside cabinet on the opposite side of the bed. Here was a top of the range Kindle, encased in a pink leather case, a half full water glass and a box of tissues. Olbeck opened the cabinet. Shoes, handbags and scarves were thrust in a piled heap within it. He began removing them, piece by piece, placing them neatly on the carpet.

"Some nice stuff here," he commented.

Kate took a look and nodded. "Well, they weren't exactly short of money, were they? They were loaded, in fact."

"Yup." Olbeck sat back on his heels and looked up at Kate. "Was that the reason for the security guard? Or was it because of MedGen?"

"Probably the latter. Don't you think? Lots of rich people around here and I don't think many of them have on-site security."

She held out a hand and pulled Olbeck up onto his feet.

"Thanks. We'll have to check."

"There's another thing," said Kate as they moved onto the next room. "Mary said the door was locked when she arrived, right?"

"Yes."

"But she didn't mention anything about turning off the alarms. She said she knew the codes, but I'm sure she didn't say anything about turning off the alarms."

Olbeck paused in the doorway to the room next to the Dorseys' bedroom.

"Yes, I think you're right. She didn't mention that, and she would have done, wouldn't she? I mean, if the alarms weren't turned off, they would have gone off after a few moments once Mary had entered the hallway, wouldn't they?"

Kate nodded.

"I would have thought so. So either they weren't turned on – why? – or they were disabled in some way, or someone who knew the codes turned them off."

"I'll flag that up to Anderton. What else? Should we try and track down the CCTV footage now, leave this search 'til later?"

Kate was touched that he was still deferring to her opinion, just as he had when they were true equals. She squeezed his arm. "I think we should. Just imagine if we can get a clear look at the perp. We could have this wrapped up by the end of the day."

Olbeck laughed a cynical laugh. "You know how much I would love to believe that. Let's go, then."

They retraced their steps back to the first room they'd come to, the conservatory at the side of the house. They could still hear the flash and whine of the cameras in the drawing room as the SOCOs continued their work.

"Where would they keep the equipment?" Olbeck asked, as he stood, hands on hips, and stared up at the ceiling, as if it would give him the answer.

Kate tapped her chin with her finger, thinking. "We should ask Mary Smith. She might know."

"Good idea."

But when they went back to the kitchen, Mary Smith had already left, carted away to the police station by Theo to make a statement. Kate shrugged when they were told by one of the uniforms.

"Well, back to looking." She looked around the room at the few people remaining. "Does anyone know where the CCTV equipment was kept?"

There were blank looks, shrugs and 'don't knows'. One dark-haired officer, who looked as if he was barely out of Hendon, volunteered the information that there were two doors in the corridor outside that might contain what they were looking for. They thanked him and made their way in the direction he'd indicated.

The corridor was tiled in ancient red floor tiles and the walls were scuffed and marked. There was a rack for wellington boots and a coat stand piled with coats and hats. Kate and Olbeck walked to the end of the corridor which terminated in a small room, stacked with cardboard boxes and odds and ends of furniture, clearly used as nothing more than a store room.

"This was probably the servants' hall, in olden times," said Kate. "Don't you think? Just off the kitchen."

"Probably." Olbeck glanced around once more and retreated back into the corridor. "How about these doors, here?"

The first door, when opened, led to a wall cupboard, but when Olbeck opened the second, he gave a satisfied chuckle. "Here we are. Good for that PC, he was right."

It was a tiny room, almost a broom cupboard, bare of furniture except for a desk on which stood a bank of blank CCTV screens. Various pieces of equipment were assembled on the top of the desk, all with a suspicious lack of electrical activity.

"Hmm." Olbeck peered over the back of the desk

and then looked at Kate with a wealth of expression on his face.

"It's turned off at the plug?" asked Kate.

"Got it in one."

"Okay..."

They looked at each other and then both suddenly laughed.

"What did I say about solving the case by the end of the day?" Kate giggled.

Olbeck pushed a hand through his hair. "Oh God, you know you jinxed it as soon as you uttered the words. If you hadn't said anything, we would have walked in here and found everything working perfectly..."

Kate looked at the blank row of screens and grew sombre again. "Wait a minute," she said. "Why the hell *are* they turned off? Why would you run a top-notch security system and not bother to switch it on?"

"Well, that's easy," said Olbeck. "Our perp turned it off. I bet he took the tapes, too."

"Tapes? Surely it would be digital?"

"Well, yes...I suppose. We'll have to get Tech to look at it. Get your mate over here, what's his name, Sam. He'll soon be able to get hold of anything, if it's there to be got."

Kate stood looking at the screens, rubbing her finger along her jaw. "The murderer knew this place," she said. "He must have done. It took us forever to find this little... cupboard. He must have known where to go."

"Not necessarily," said Olbeck. "We have no idea about times, at this point. He could have been here all night, searched the whole house...although—" He stopped for a minute. "You're right, in a way. It's a hell of a risk to come all this way, with this many cameras, on the off chance that you *might* be able to disable them."

"Exactly."

They both stood looking at the dead equipment in front of them for a moment longer, as if it would suddenly, spontaneously, spring into life again. Then, almost as one, they turned and said, "Let's get going, then," half laughed at their timing, and left the room, Olbeck shutting the door firmly behind him.

Chapter Ten

STUART WAS BACK AT THE protest the next morning and was unsurprised to see that neither James or Rosie, or even Angie, had made it. Sleeping off massive hangovers, probably. He introduced himself to the middle-aged lady who was behind the leaflet table, whose name was Jane. It was a cold day, with intermittent spitting rain, and no one came along to question or harangue them. After twenty minutes, Stuart decided that he'd be better off, chasing up his new friends.

Back at his car, he mused over which direction to take. Almost without hesitation, he decided on the direction of the squat. As he drove there, he was uncomfortably aware of just how much he wanted to see Angie. He reflected on what had happened the night before in some disbelief. He would never have thought that he would go that far, actually sleep with someone he had under observation. He was half proud of himself, half aghast. He wanted to tell someone, just to share the secret; that particular secret amongst all the secrets he was having to keep, but he knew that he couldn't. Who would he tell, anyway? Anderton? His boss? Aloud, he scoffed, shook his head and dismissed the thought. By the time he parked the car outside the scruffy house, he was firmly back into character.

He wanted to walk straight in but caution made him ring the doorbell and, when that failed to work, knock on the peeling paint of the front door. After a wait of a few minutes, it was opened by a man – a boy, really – someone who Stuart had never seen before, with curly auburn hair, a half-asleep expression and dressed only in a dirty T-shirt and boxer shorts.

"Is Angie in?"

"What?" said the boy, scratching his neck. Then his expression cleared. "Oh, you're Mike, aren't you? Angie said you might be coming."

Stuart felt a tremor of something: anxiety, or was it anticipation? "She's in, then?"

"Yeah. Upstairs." He said nothing else but stood back to let Stuart into the house.

Stuart climbed the stairs to Angie's glittering cave. He expected to find her lolling in bed, possibly naked, but she was standing in the middle of the room, dressed in a white vest and black combat trousers, feet in laced up black plimsolls. She looked... *alive*, that was the first word that sprang to mind. To Stuart's eyes, the air around her shimmered for a moment and the casual cocky grin he was wearing dropped off his face within seconds.

She fixed him with her gaze, her face back to its beautiful blank mask again. Then she smiled and the odd moment of tension was broken.

"Hello, you," she said, quite casually.

"Hi." Stuart hesitated for a second, crossed the room and took her into his arms. She returned his kiss briefly but voraciously.

"Were you going out?" he asked, when he could breathe again.

"I was," said Angie. "It can wait, though."

This shouldn't be happening, thought Stuart, even as their clothes fell to the floor. This shouldn't be happening. I have to stop it. But still he was on the bed with her, under the covers with her, even while he was saying that to himself. I have to stop it, this can't go on... but then it was useless, the words dropped away and there wasn't room for any thought at all.

Afterwards, she lay face down with her head turned from him. He ran a hand down her back, marvelling at the perfection of her skin, that whiteness dusted with golden freckles. He thought she'd fallen asleep and was surprised when she spoke.

"Where do you live?"

"London," Stuart said, briefly. Always stick as closely to the true facts as you can. Angie made an indeterminate noise. "Have you lived here long?" he asked.

"'Bout six months." Angie turned her head to look at him and he was struck anew by the perfection of her features. She could be a model, he thought, opened his mouth to tell her and then firmly shut it again, cringing at the thought. What was the matter with him?

"Where did you live before?"

Angie shrugged with one shoulder. "With a friend."

She said it in a neutral tone but Stuart was surprised at the sudden spurt of jealousy he felt. Better get over that, and quickly...

"So, when you're not protesting, what do you do?" he asked, changing the subject

"I'm an artist."

Inwardly Stuart rolled his eyes. Of course she was. "What kind of art? Paintings, you mean?"

Angie smiled. "All sorts of art. Multi-media, mostly. Digital and video, and sound combined with physical media."

"Right," said Stuart, none the wiser.

Angie's mouth quirked up at the corner. "This room is one of my works, you know."

Stuart looked around him. The curtains were shut and the mirror pieces glittered dimly through the half-darkness.

"It's a piece of work, all right." He raised an arm

slowly and lowered it, watching the infinite tiny reflections in the mirror pieces. Angie rested her head on her arm and watched him, still smiling.

"You know they say that you shouldn't get between two mirrors," she said. "It's bad luck."

"Why?" asked Stuart, still watching his arm in the mirrors.

Angie rolled onto her back. "I don't know. Perhaps because it drags out a piece of your soul."

"Right," said Stuart, grinning. "I'll risk it."

"Well, you have to have a soul in the first place."

"Is that right?" asked Stuart. "Are you saying I don't?"

She shook her head, smiling that closed, secretive smile again. "No, you're all right," she said. Then she said, in the same voice, "I don't have one."

"One what?"

"A soul." She rolled to face him. They were eye to eye for a breathless, hushed moment while her words reverberated around the silent room. Then Stuart laughed and Angie laughed and the tension was broken.

"So," said Stuart, keeping his tone very casual, "How did you get mixed up with all the protests, then?"

Angie kept her eyes fixed on him. She smiled a little. "Mixed up?"

"Yeah. I mean, how did you get into it in the first place?"

Angie's smile grew wider. "I think you're labouring under a bit of a misapprehension," she said and giggled a little. "I'm not part of the protest. I don't – I'm not into that sort of thing."

"You're not?" Stuart could feel the half smile on his face sag into non-existence. "So how come—"

"I know James and Rosie? I just do. We have a lot of parties."

"Oh, right. So protesting's not really your thing, then?"

Angie rolled onto her back again and yawned. "No. I don't care enough about it. All I care about is—" She stopped for a moment and brushed away a strand of hair from her face. "I just want to make art. That's all that really matters to me."

"Good for you," Stuart said automatically, while his mind sifted through this new information. Topmost was the thought, sudden and inescapable, was that if this were true, he had no need of Angie's company, anymore. He was disconcerted by the sudden jump of anxiety, of grief almost, that that engendered in him.

Get a grip, Stuart. You're playing a dangerous game, here.

"I could show you my portfolio, if you like," said Angie. The diffidence of her voice touched him.

"I'd like that," Stuart said. Then, wanting to escape the clamouring voices in his head, telling him to leave, get out of there, try something else, he pulled her closer to him and kissed her.

EN ROUTE TO THE HOSPITAL, Kate felt her phone buzz and jitter. A text from Andrew, asking if she was coming back to his house later. She realised, with a guilty jump of the heart, that she hadn't spared him a second's thought since she'd left him that morning. Could it really still be the same day? It felt as though a week had passed since that peaceful breakfast in his conservatory. It was only then that Kate remembered his suggestion that she move in with him. She swallowed, put the phone back in her bag without answering it and turned her mind from the problem.

On arrival at the hospital, they were directed up to the Intensive Care Unit. There, they found Anderton pacing up and down in the reception area. He raised his eyebrows as they walked towards him, but Kate couldn't read his expression. Did that mean Madeline Dorsey was still alive?

The smell of the hospital, a nostril-flaring mix of disinfectant, old sweat and worse, brought Kate back to that time last summer, after the incident. She tried to think of it as *the incident*, not *the time I almost died*; it helped, somehow. It reduced its importance in her mind. She remembered those first confused and pain-filled weeks and then the long, slow process of recovery; endless physiotherapy appointments, counselling sessions, too many afternoons spent on her sofa watching crappy romantic comedies and anything that didn't involve violence or bloodshed. Too many nights waking up with a sodden pillowcase, coming back to consciousness with a start, clasping her chest and gasping for air. She never dreamed directly about her attacker; instead she was attacked by birds with long sharp beaks, impaled by metal poles, or she fell endlessly towards spiked railings.

"Kate?"

She realised she'd come to a standstill in the middle of the room and blinked, bringing herself back to the present. Anderton and Olbeck were both regarding her with curiosity, tinged with a little concern. She forced a smile. "Just thinking," she said. "Is there any news?"

Anderton looked sombre. "Nothing definite. The docs are not holding out much hope, though, from what little I've been able to glean."

Nothing of the ward could be seen through the opaque glass panels of the swing doors. Kate could picture Madeline Dorsey though, flat on her back on a hospital gurney, tubes and pipes and needles festooning her body. Hanging by her fingernails from a precipice, oblivion in the abyss underneath. *Hold on, Madeline.* Would she drop to join Jack

Dorsey, or cling on for her children? Which would it be?

Occasionally, a harassed-looking doctor or nurse would hurry through the doors or past the windows of the ward. Kate knew her job was stressful, but it didn't compare to the working conditions of these people. No wonder Andrew had opted for pathology; not for the physically squeamish, true, but you didn't have to confront the kind of messy human emotions that a doctor to the living would have to deal with on a day to day basis. Thinking of Andrew, she checked her phone, reading his message again. Even as she was contemplating a reply, another text came through from him, repeating his former question. For the first time, Kate was conscious of a surge of annoyance. After a moment, she texted back *sorry, still on case, will be totally shattered so will head to mine. Call you later.* After another moment, she added a kiss to the end of the message and sent it. Then she turned her phone off and put it away.

After another hour's wait, there was still no news. Anderton began to mutter about getting back to the office. Kate volunteered to stay.

"Sure?" asked Anderton.

Kate nodded. Olbeck opted to go back with Anderton. As the two men left, they passed a woman in the doorway, a blonde, dressed in a white linen shirt and blue jeans, with long legs that ended in feet tucked into jewelled sandals. Her face was pretty but terribly drawn, her eyes red and her mouth pulled in tight. She was breathing fast, as if she'd been running. Kate watched her walk to the doorway of the ICU and hover, clasping her arms across her body. Then the woman turned, saw Kate watching her and came towards her.

"I don't know what's happening," she said, her voice ragged with panic. "Why won't somebody tell me what's happening to Madeline?"

Kate got up immediately. "You know Madeline Dorsey?" she asked.

The woman nodded, a quick bob of the head as if her neck were stiff. "I'm her sister. Harriet Larsen." She eyed Kate with confusion. "Who are you?"

Kate introduced herself and Harriet blanched. For a second, Kate was sure she was going to faint and quickly grabbed Harriet's arm, steering her over to the bank of chairs at the side of the room.

"Thanks," said Harriet faintly, when she was safely seated. "I'm sorry, I just don't know what to think – I can hardly take it in. Is it – is it true that Jack's *dead*?"

Kate hesitated. Then she said, "There's been no formal identification just yet, but yes, I'm afraid he is."

Harriet drew in her breath in a whooping gasp. She put one hand up to her trembling mouth, pearly painted nails pressed against her lips.

"Dead..." she whispered, half to herself. Then she cried, big ragged sobs, dropping her head so her blonde hair fell forward in a long, fair curtain.

Kate sat down next to her and kept a hand on Harriet's arm. She let her cry for a few minutes and then gave her arm a comforting little squeeze. It was hard, she supposed, to question someone in the depths of extreme emotional torment, but the truth was that, when someone was emotionally vulnerable, it was sometimes when you could learn some very valuable things. And time, naturally, was always of the essence. She waited for a slight cessation in Harriet's tears and then, after murmuring a few words of condolence, she said "This must be terribly hard for you, Harriet, I'm so sorry. But if you could talk to me now, tell me about Jack and Madeline, it would really help. We need all the information we can get, if we're going to catch the person who did this."

Harriet sobbed harder. Kate said, slightly more firmly. "Do you understand?"

After a moment, there was a bob of the head. Then Harriet raised her tear-stained face. "Yes, I understand," she said, hoarsely. "What – what do you want to know?"

"Well," said Kate. "Let's start at the beginning. You're Madeline's sister, right? Older or younger?"

"I'm the oldest. Madeline's two years younger than I am."

"Do you have any other siblings?"

"No. It's just us."

"What about your parents?"

Harriet gave another gasping breath that was almost a sob. "Mum died about ten years ago. Oh, thank God she's been spared this, thank God... she couldn't have coped. Dad lives overseas. I've spoken to him, he knows... he's trying to get a flight over here—"

"Where does he live?"

"Denmark. Copenhagen. He's half Danish, you see, and after Mum died he went back to live there."

Kate nodded, thinking that explained the sisters' fairness and height. "Did you grow up there?"

Harriet shook that long fair mane of hair again. "No, no we always lived in England. Up North, actually, near Harrogate."

"Where did Madeline meet Jack?"

A little colour was coming back into Harriet's face. She sat up a little. "University. They met at Oxford. Madeline was doing English and Jack was doing something very scientific. Particle physics, or something like that. Well, maybe not physics. I never actually understood it and he tried to explain it to me about three times." Harriet was almost smiling. Then memory obviously returned and her face fell apart again. She raised a trembling hand to her mouth. "I can't believe he's dead, I can't *believe* it. Who would have hurt him? Everyone liked him..."

Her voice was dissolving. Kate said quickly, "So Madeline and Jack met at Oxford. That's where Jack met his business partner too, isn't it?"

"Alex? Yes, that's right." Harriet cleared her throat. "They were in the same halls in the first year, had the rooms next to one another." Something seemed to strike her and she turned to Kate, wide-eyed. "God – *Alex* – has anyone told him? Does he know? He'll be devastated, he was Jack's best friend…"

"Don't worry about that," said Kate, patting Harriet's arm. "We'll keep everyone informed, as well as we can. So you've known Jack and Alex since they were at university?"

Harriet nodded. She took a deep breath. "Yes, we've all known each other a long time. Almost like family, you know?" She was on the verge of saying more when they were interrupted by the appearance of an exhausted looking doctor. Harriet jumped up, her face grey.

"Is she – oh my god, is she—"

"Madeline's in a critical condition, Ms Larsen, but we've done what we can for her." The doctor looked at Kate with raised eyebrows and she introduced herself quickly, flashing her card. He gave it a cursory glance and then turned his attention back to Harriet. "As I was saying, she's as stable as she can possibly be at the moment. I won't pretend to you that her condition is not very serious, very serious indeed, but at the moment, she's holding on."

Harriet sat back down on the plastic chair abruptly. She looked up at the doctor, her face working, hope and despair battling it out for control of her features. "Will she – will she live?"

The doctor half smiled. "She's doing as well as she can, Ms Larsen. You must – you must prepare yourself, though. I simply can't give you that reassurance at this time. I'm sorry."

Harriet dropped her head, nodding minutely. Kate caught the doctor's arm as he was turning away.

"A quick word?" She drew him a little away from Harriet. "I have to ask you to restrict access to Mrs Dorsey," she said. "No admittance to anyone apart from medical staff, okay?"

"Naturally," snapped the doctor. He was a grey-haired man of about fifty and he looked rather outraged, as if Kate were trying to tell him his job. "That goes without saying, Officer."

"Fine," said Kate. "I'll have a uniformed officer here when I leave."

"As you wish. Now, if you'll excuse me..."

Kate watched him walk back into the ICU. Then she returned to Harriet, who was staring blankly at the floor. "Let me get you a cup of tea, Harriet," she said. "And you can carry on with what you were telling me."

Chapter Eleven

"Morning, team," Anderton said the next morning, crashing through the door in his usual ebullient fashion. Kate, Olbeck, Theo, Rav and Jane were ranged around the office, talking amongst themselves. Kate, noticing the empty chair that stood at her old desk, wondered what Stuart was doing and whether he was making any progress. For a moment, she considered what it must be like to work under cover. Having to pretend to be someone else, day in and day out. I'd be a natural at it, she thought, with a wry inner grin. That's what I've been doing since the start of my career.

Her thought process was derailed by Anderton slapping another crime scene photograph on the whiteboard. It was a hugely magnified shot of the word left written in blood at the scene. Kate read it again, remembering the room and the heavy, wet scent of blood in the air. *Killer*. She wondered what Anderton had to say.

"Firstly," he began, hoisting himself onto the

edge of a spare desk. "You'll be glad to know that Madeline Dorsey continues to hang on. She's still in intensive care and she's in an incredibly bad way. I don't think we'll be taking any witness statements from her any time soon, but she *is* still alive, so we'll just have to wait and see. Kate, you spoke to her sister at the hospital, didn't you? Anything there we should know about?"

Kate pushed her fringe back from her face. "Her name's Harriet Larsen and she's the older sister by two years. No other siblings, their mother is dead and their father lives abroad in Denmark. He's been informed and I think he's probably already in the country, by now. Harriet's known Jack Dorsey and Alexander Hargreaves since they – Jack and Madeline – met at Oxford, over twenty years ago. She was too distressed to tell me much more than that, but as far as she was aware, the Dorseys had a good relationship. She wasn't aware of anything out of the ordinary, in terms of strange visitors, odd happenings, etcetera etcetera, but she doesn't live locally, she's London-based and she hadn't seen her sister for a couple of months."

Anderton nodded. "Did she say they were close? Did they talk a lot? Would Madeline have confided in her?"

Kate shrugged. "I'm going back to talk to her again, later today. Hope to get a bit deeper this time."

"Okay, good." Anderton jumped from the desk and began pacing in front of the whiteboards. "Now, we're still waiting on a lot of the forensics and the PM on Dorsey won't take place until tomorrow. I think your beau might be doing that, Kate." He grinned, as did Theo and Olbeck. Kate tried to smile, but was conscious of a spurt of something much like humiliation. Why did Anderton think it was such a bloody big joke that she had a boyfriend? "Anyway, Mark, can you pop along and see what's what when that goes ahead?"

Olbeck nodded. Anderton reached the wall and turned on his heel to retrace his steps. "Kate, I want you to come with me while I go and see young Mister Hargreaves. I want his alibi checked."

He raised a hand. "Standard procedure, people. Don't go jumping to conclusions. The same goes for Harriet Larsen, Madeline's father, the cleaner, and any other staff in the house." Anderton came to a halt and a brief silence fell. "I'm not sure about this one," he said quietly. There was an odd, loaded hush in the room. Every eye was fixed upon him. "There's a few too many undercurrents here for my liking. Is this another terrorist attack? Or is there something else going on? I don't know. And I know you lot don't know, but that's what we have to find out. I know we can do it. I know *you* can do it."

Kate was suddenly conscious that she was sitting up straighter, shoulders back, like a soldier on parade. How did Anderton *do* that? Look at us all, she thought, watching the others. We'd go into battle for him. I know I would.

Anderton clapped his hands together and the sharp noise broke the spell. He crooked his finger at Kate and she nodded and jumped up, grabbing her coat and bag. She gave Olbeck a wave and then followed her boss from the room.

It wasn't until she was sitting in the passenger seat next to Anderton that she realised that, essentially, this was the first time she and he had been alone together since... well, since that night. Immediately, memories and images recurred and she fumbled with the seatbelt, keeping her head down while she clicked it into place to hide the blush that wanted to surface on her face. Then she smoothed her hair back and sat up, in control of herself again.

"Well, Kate," Anderton said as he accelerated away from the station. "Here we are. How are you feeling?"

He couldn't know what she'd just been thinking of, could he? Was he remembering the same thing? Kate coughed.

"Sorry," she said. "I'm fine. I'm back in the swing of it, now."

"Well, it's certainly back in the deep end, isn't it?"

"You're not wrong. Still, I may as well start as I mean to go on."

Anderton smiled. They waited to join the traffic on the dual carriageway.

It was a day of oddly contrasting weather; brilliant sunshine one moment, spitting rain and scudding grey clouds the next. The car windscreen wipers went on, then off, then on again. By the time they reached the driveway that led to Hargreaves' house, the grey clouds had closed completely overhead, the sky like a dingy flannel blanket that sagged ominously with oncoming rain. The driveway led through pine woods, the trees in regimented lines, obviously an old plantation. Now and again, Kate could see patches of sandy heath in the distance with the spiky shapes of the gorse bushes and the softer outline of heather. The road plunged back into the dimness of the pine forest again, wound gently through the trees, and eventually came out in front of a large and unusual looking house. Part of it looked much older than the other, a square stone building that had been absorbed into a much more modern construction of wooden frames, cedar cladding and large glass windows. The windows ran in a long, unbroken line of glass that stretched around the side of the house, and onto a large wooden jetty and decking area which skirted the edge of a lake.

It looked deserted, although a silver BMW was

parked near the front door. Kate and Anderton got out of their own car. The wind gusted through the pine trees on the edge of the shore and Kate could hear the faint lapping of water against the jetty. Overhead came the shrill shriek of some sort of bird of prey. These were the only sounds she could hear and she was reminded of arriving at Jack Dorsey's house on the day after the murder – how silent it had been. For a moment, she felt a ridiculous jump of panic. Were they going to open the front door to find Alex Hargreaves' body, face down in a pool of blood or stabbed so viciously he was unrecognisable?

She told herself not to be so stupid, but she could see Anderton was a little uneasy, too. He glanced towards the silent house, with its blank, shuttered look.

"They like their out of the way retreats," he murmured. "Look at it. You couldn't be much more isolated."

"I know," said Kate. "I guess if you can afford it..."

"What I don't understand is—" Anderton began, and then they both started a little as the front door swung open. For a moment, the doorway showed only blackness and then the tall figure of Alexander Hargreaves moved into the light. He was wearing dark glasses and his expression could not be discerned. After a minute glance at one another, Kate and Anderton approached him.

"I know why you've come," he said in a flat voice.

"You've been informed of the death of Jack Dorsey?" Anderton said and Hargreaves winced.

"The people who broke it to me the first time were a bit more tactful," he said, but in the same flat voice, with no real heat in the reproachful words. He turned away from them and walked back into the house, almost plodding, leaving the door open behind him. Kate and Anderton followed him through the doorway and Kate shut the door behind them.

The interior of the house was large and airy, the wooden beams supporting the roof used as an architectural feature. The floor was tiled in slate, the furniture uncompromisingly modern. There was a lot of leather and glass about, and quite a variety of modern art. Kate's eye was caught by a sculpture that looked like an elongated robot, all twisted silver limbs and square protrusions. Then she noticed a framed painting on the far wall which looked like, and quite possibly was, a genuine Jackson Pollock.

Hargreaves had slumped down on one of the large leather couches. On the glass table in front of him was a square cut-crystal glass, half full of an amber-coloured liquid.

"I don't suppose either of you want a drink," he

said, a statement more than a question. Kate and Anderton confirmed his presumption with a shake of their heads. He gave the ghost of a nod and went on, "Well, I'm sure you won't mind if I have one. I need one, by God."

"This must be very distressing for you—" Anderton began and was interrupted by Hargreaves' gasp, a half sob that shook his rigid shoulders. He put a hand up to his mouth, as if holding himself back from retching. As Kate watched, tears began to slide out from under his dark glasses and, a few moments later, Hargreaves removed them, throwing them down on the table next to his whiskey glass. His eyes were red-rimmed and puffy.

"I can't take it in," he said after a moment, in a ragged voice. He rubbed the tears away from his face. "I never thought... Jack – and Madeline too... I can't – I can't bear it..."

Kate cleared her throat, glanced at Anderton for permission. "Mrs Dorsey is still alive," she said quietly.

Hargreaves head snapped up. A variety of emotions chased themselves over his face. "Is that true?" he breathed, as if talking louder would draw a negative response from Kate. "Seriously? She's still alive?"

Kate nodded. Anderton said "She's alive but she's still extremely ill. There's a good chance that she won't make it. I'm sorry."

Hargreaves' eyes filled with tears again and he dropped his head into his hands. "Why would you say that?" he muttered. "Why give me that hope and then take it away again?"

"She's doing as well as she can, sir," said Kate, feeling a wrench of pity. "The doctors are doing all they can do. Her sister and father are with her."

Hargreaves raised his head again. "Harriet's here? I must call her – she must be devastated, poor girl. They were close..."

There was a moment's silence. After another glance from Anderton, Kate leant forward a little. "We'd like to talk to you about Jack and Madeline, if we may, sir. You might be able to give us some more information that could be very valuable."

"Me?" Hargreaves rubbed his face again. "I don't know what I can tell you."

You were only his friend and partner for twenty years, thought Kate impatiently. If you can't tell us anything, then we're really in trouble.

Anderton had clearly been thinking the same thing. He said, with a slight edge to his voice, "The first thing you can tell us, sir, is where you were between the hours of eleven pm and two am on the night of Thursday the ninth of May."

Hargreaves blinked his sore-looking eyelids rapidly. "You want to know where I was that – that night? Why, for God's sake? You can't seriously suspect me of killing my friend?"

His tone was verging on panic-stricken. Anderton raised a placatory hand. "Standard procedure, sir. We ask everyone. It's a process of elimination, nothing more."

Hargreaves continued to blink rapidly. "I was – I was – where the hell was I?" He still sounded panicky. "I'm sorry, my nerves are shot to pieces... that's right, I was at the pub. In the village." Relief flooded his voice. "There's a good gastro-pub in the village, I eat there quite a lot. I was there most of the night, ran into a few buddies, played some pool after dinner. The Haverton Arms, in the village."

"I see," said Kate, writing down the name. "And what time did you leave?"

"Late... I don't know exactly. It's got a late licence. I don't know – maybe one o'clock? One thirty?"

"Did you drive there?"

"I never drive there," said Hargreaves, in a virtuous tone. "Always want a drink, you see, and it's not too far. I can cut back across my land."

"Were you alone?"

"Yes." Now he sounded offended. "What do you mean?"

"I don't mean anything, sir. Do you have a partner? A wife?"

"I'm divorced," said Hargreaves heavily. "Not that I can see the relevance of that to this situation. I got divorced about five years ago and I've been fancy-free and single ever since."

131

"You've known Jack Dorsey a good few years, isn't that right?" Anderton asked.

Hargreaves nodded. He reached out, picked up his drink with one hand and his dark glasses with the other. He took a sip of whiskey and swung the glasses by their arm.

"Jack and I met at university," he said. "Oxford. We had rooms side by side and somehow we just – well, we just clicked, really. Chalk and cheese, you know – don't know why we clicked but we did..." He trailed off into silence.

Kate took up the questions. "Had you or Mr Dorsey ever received any threats?" she asked. "Any direct threats, or even implied ones? By letter, or email or in person?"

Hargreaves gave her an incredulous look. "Are you serious?" he asked. "We were threatened *all the time*. We never opened any of our post, it all went through Security and was X-rayed. We've both got unregistered numbers, both careful... but – I don't know – until that car bomb, it never felt very real, if you know what I mean. Just a load of animal rights nutters and old biddies. We never actually felt like they'd actually do us any harm."

"Both you and Mr Dorsey live in extremely isolated conditions," said Anderton, in a neutral tone. "For people who were worried about security, that does strike me as rather strange."

Hargreaves half laughed. "Really?" he asked.

"It makes perfect sense to me. It did to Jack. Hide yourself away and you won't be bothered. We've both got serious security systems, I mean, really top notch ones."

Kate and Anderton exchanged glances.

"That didn't seem to do Mr Dorsey much good, in the end," Anderton said eventually.

Hargreaves winced again and dropped his head. "I don't know," he said. "I don't know what happened there. Jack had a security guard, for God's sake—"

"Who is also dead," Anderton went on, remorselessly.

"I don't know," repeated Hargreaves. He was shaking his head from side to side, as if to clear his thoughts. "I don't know how it could have happened."

They left him pouring another glass of whiskey while they took a short walk around the outside of the house, ostensibly to check on his own security arrangements. Kate and Anderton stood side by side on the decking looking over the surface of the lake, its waters ruffled into a multitude of little wavelets by the wind. It was beautiful, undeniably, but there was something lonely, something almost sinister in the landscape, empty of any sign of human activity. Kate thought of being here in the dark, alone, with the night pressing heavily against that great expanse of glass and almost shivered. The lapping of the water against the pillars of the decking was almost hypnotic. Kate found herself staring at a bobble of floating litter trapped against one of the pillars; several screwed up balls of pink paper, a crumpled plastic bag and an empty juice bottle. She focused her eyes on the up and down movement as her mind ticked over what they'd just heard.

"Let's check his alibi on the way back," said Anderton. "We might have a spot of lunch there, if the food is as good as Hargreaves says it is. What do you think?"

They easily found the pub in the village. Part of it was obviously the original building, probably dating back to Tudor times, judging from the broad black beams that ran through the walls, and when they entered it, the pitted stone floor and low ceilings. The windows were mullioned and small. A larger, modern extension had been built onto it, to house the restaurant. Kate had expected Anderton to quiz the staff about Alex Hargreaves' presence on the night of the murder, but he shook his head when she asked and directed her to a table.

"Let's eat, first," he said, with a grin. "I get nervous when I have my food prepared by someone who knows I'm a copper. You never know when they might hold a grudge."

Kate smiled. They found a table by the fireplace which held a vase of silk flowers. Kate relaxed back into her easy chair. Looking around, she realised that this was exactly the sort of place she liked to eat: comfortable, quietly decorated, people dressed casually, talking and laughing without much reserve. The waitress was a large young woman, with a cheerful face and spiky blonde pigtails. A secondary thought followed the first; she really didn't much like the formal restaurants she went to with Andrew – all those hovering, deferential, attentive waiters, the hush that fell over the room that seemed to muffle any attempt at a normal conversation. She was always worried about spilling something on the white linen tablecloths. Kate looked across at Anderton who was reading a menu and commenting enthusiastically on various dishes. Shit, this really did feel like a date. She dragged her own attention back to the menu, her appetite deserting her.

"So," said Anderton, once their food had arrived and they were eating; Kate without much enthusiasm. "How's it feel to be back at work?"

Kate chewed, giving herself time to formulate an appropriate answer. "Fine."

"You're not finding it a bit much? Straight back into a serious murder investigation?"

"No," Kate said, a bit annoyed. She was getting a bit tired of being treated like some fragile, porcelain doll. "I don't find it a problem at all."

"Okay. Just asking."

"Sorry," said Kate. "It's just – oh, I don't know – I get a bit fed up of all this solicitousness."

"I thought you'd be glad people cared," said Anderton.

Their eyes met across the table and Kate was transported back to that one night, a year before, instantly. Damn it, when was she going to get over that? The worst thing was that she could see Anderton was thinking along much the same lines.

There was a moment of loaded silence. Kate was very aware that they were eating in a pub that offered accommodation as well. We could do it, she thought. We could book a room here, just for the night, and stay a few hours. No one would know. She felt giddy with the possibility, almost faint with the longing. I just need to say it and he'll agree.

Oddly, it was the thought of Olbeck's face, if he ever found out, that stopped her. She pictured his shock, her shame and embarrassment... Andrew's face came into her mind a few moments later and then, of course, she was swamped by guilt at him not being the first thing that stopped her.

She stood up abruptly. "Want another drink?"

Anderton indicated their half full glasses. "What's wrong with yours?"

Kate blinked and sat down again. "Oh. Yes. Sorry."

"Are you all right?"

He sounded merely concerned. Perhaps she'd imagined that look in his eyes. Thank God she hadn't done anything about it. Kate realised something –

that there couldn't be any more of these cosy little meals together. Not alone. She wouldn't always be able to be strong.

The plump waitress came to see if they wanted anything else and Kate could have kissed her. Anderton replied in the negative to her enquiry, but then followed it up with "But you could help us with something else, if you don't mind."

Anderton pulled a print out of Alexander Hargreaves' headshot from the MedGen website and held it out.

"Can you tell me if you know this man?"

"Alex?" said the waitress. "Seriously, are you, like, joking? He's in here all the time."

"You definitely recognise him?"

"Oh yeah. He's often in here to eat and play the fruit machines."

"Was he here last Thursday night? The ninth of May?"

The waitress narrowed her eyes in suspicion, which then widened as Anderton showed her his warrant card. "Oh," she said. "Right. Yeah. Yeah, he was here then."

"Do you know what time he left?"

"Not sure. Quite late. Sometimes he stays behind for a bit, after we close up. It's like a private party," she added, hastily, as if they were going to arrest her for breaking the licensing laws.

Anderton nodded. "You have CCTV here?" he asked.

The waitress looked positively scared now. "Yeah, we do. Above the front door."

"Could we perhaps speak to the manager?" asked Kate, smiling reassuringly. "What's his name?"

"Tim," the waitress said, one finger up to her pierced lip. "Tim Jones. I'll go and get him, shall I?"

She hurried off before they could speak. Anderton gave a tiny shrug and turned his attention back to his plate. Kate stared after the girl for a moment. The ring in the waitress's lip had reminded her of someone.

"How's Stuart getting on?"

Anderton looked up in surprise. "Stuart? Fine, as far as I know. We'll pull him in for a debrief soon, but he's been reporting in regularly."

"Hmm."

Anderton finished the last mouthful on his plate and pushed it away from him with a satisfied sigh. "You don't like him, do you?"

Kate half-laughed. "I don't even know him."

"Well," said Anderton. "We none of us really know him. I know he's good at his job, and that's exactly the sort of person I needed."

Kate placed her knife and fork together neatly in the centre of her plate. "Who is he, really?" she asked.

Anderton met her gaze steadily. "SO15, Kate. You know that, I don't need to spell it out."

"Why? Why go that far?"

"I had to, Kate. We're out of our depth, here. I need someone on the inside and my team aren't – you people aren't trained for it and you're too well known around here. I needed an outsider, someone with experience." He pushed his chair back a little and added "Someone who knows what he's doing."

Kate smoothed back her hair. "We were out of our depth last year," she said. "You said that. We still got a solve."

"*You* got a solve," said Anderton. "No one's forgetting that."

Kate forcibly restrained her hand from reaching around to rub her back. She saw Anderton's eyes flick downward at the sudden, stilled movement of her hand and was sure he knew exactly what she was trying to stop herself doing.

"I'm fine," she hissed suddenly, as if he'd just told her the opposite.

"I—"Anderton began, but they were interrupted by arrival of the manager of the pub; a tall, gangly young man with anxious eyebrows.

Tim Jones looked barely out of his teens but he grasped what they wanted with speed. After leading them to a viewing room, which reminded Kate a little of the one at Jack Dorsey's house, they could see for themselves a grainy black and white image of Alex Hargreaves entering the pub at eight thirty five pm on the ninth of May and leaving it again, slightly unsteadily, at one forty one am that night.

"Well," said Kate as they drove away. "He's out. What now?"

"Dorsey's PM is tomorrow. We need to interview Harriet Larsen and I need an update from the hospital, see if our Madeline is still holding on."

"I'll do Harriet," offered Kate.

"Good, okay. Take Theo with you."

"Okay," Kate said, suppressing a groan. She looked at Anderton's profile. That moment of weakness back in the pub dining room seemed even more like madness to her now. She pulled out her mobile and texted Andrew; *miss you, shall I come round to yours tonight?* She signed it off with three kisses.

Chapter Twelve

STUART PUT ANGIE'S DRINK DOWN in front of her on the scarred top of the pub table. She was busying texting someone on her phone and was so intent on the task that she barely looked up.

"'Thanks, Mike,'" Stuart said ironically when she finally slipped the phone into her pocket.

"Thanks," Angie said, not rising to the bait. She took a deep swallow of the whiskey and said nothing more.

Stuart sipped his pint. This was the first time he and Angie had been out together, to a pub of her choice. Stuart didn't think much of it – it was scruffy, down-at-heel, with a variety of rough looking men congregating at the bar. Angie didn't seem to notice the squalor. She sipped her drink, looking out the grimy window by the table, her eyes fixed on something that Stuart couldn't see. Again, she was dressed only in black and white.

"Don't you ever wear any colours?" asked Stuart, if nothing else but to break the silence.

Angie seemed to come back to life. She turned to face him, smiling. "Why do you ask?"

"I only ever see you wearing black and white clothes. Is it deliberate, or—"

"Yes, I suppose you could say it's deliberate," said Angie, slowly, as if she'd not considered the matter before. She tapped the side of her head. "All the colour's up here, you see. It's all there and it only comes out in my work."

Stuart didn't know why but he felt awkward when she mentioned anything to do with art. It was pretentious, that was why; it was something that felt phony, unreal. Listen to yourself, he chided himself. Who are you to talk about being false?

He felt impatient – at her, at himself. He was supposed to be on a case, he was supposed to be gathering information. Instead he was sat here, in a shit pub, with someone who wasn't even really part of the scene he was supposed to be investigating. And if he was just going to sit here in silence with Angie, with her occasionally waffling nonsense about 'art', then he'd quite frankly rather be in bed with her, not talking...

He stamped down on his impatience.

"Where did you grow up?" he asked, leaning forward and taking her hand. She had small hands, unvarnished nails edged with occasional rainbow rims of paint.

Angie looked at him. Some indefinable emotion

passed over her face in a flicker too quick to gauge. "Guildford," she said briefly.

"I know it," said Stuart. "Do your parents still live there?"

"They don't live there."

"But—"

"I said that's where I grew up. That's not where my parents lived."

"So," said Stuart, confused. "What are you say—"

"I grew up in care," said Angie. She withdrew her hand from his.

"Well," said Stuart in a hearty tone that even he despised. "There's nothing wrong with that."

"There's plenty wrong with that," said Angie. "My mother died when I was little and when I was ten, my father remarried. My stepmother hated me and my father took her side."

"Oh," said Stuart. "That must have been hard." He felt like hitting his forehead sharply. What a stupid thing to say...

"Yes," said Angie remotely. She swallowed the rest of her drink.

"Want another?"

"Yes."

Stuart went to the bar and got another couple of drinks. When he got back to the table, Angie had gone.

Flabbergasted, he stood for a moment with the drinks in his hands. Then he spotted her through the grimy window. She was pacing up and down, talking on her mobile. The walls were too thick and the wind outside was too strong for him to hear what she was saying. As he watched, still clutching his glasses, she ended the call and turned back to the door of the pub. Quickly, he sat down at the table.

She sat down again without comment, picked up her fresh drink and drained it in three gulps. She didn't thank him.

"Are you all right?" asked Stuart.

She gave him a brief, chilly smile. "I'm fine," she said. "I've got to go. See you later."

"Wait—" Stuart said, but his only answer was the pub door banging shut behind her. He sat there for a while, finishing his own drink. What on Earth was that all about? This is stupid, he told himself. Why are you even bothering with her? He tossed the last remaining mouthful of his drink back and jumped up. Sod her, then. It was time to get back to work.

MADELINE DORSEY CONTINUED TO CLING to life. Kate had phoned the hospital before she went to see Harriet Larsen. The prognosis remained the same but, for now, she was alive. Kate swung the car into the car park of the hotel that Harriet was staying in, one of the nicest ones in Abbeyford. She'd called round for Theo but he'd already taken off to re-interview the security guard at the MedGen facility. Kate supposed she should be feeling aggrieved, rather than relieved.

Kate walked into the foyer of the hotel. As old and stately as it looked on the outside, the inside was almost aggressively modern in décor, with a lot of leather, glass and chrome in evidence. Kate was briefly reminded of Alex Hargreaves' house. She found Harriet Larsen in one of the sitting rooms, at the back of the hotel, where a long glassed-in enclosure got the best of the morning sunlight. It was a peaceful place, with comfortable chairs dotted about low tables, gentle jazz music playing on some kind of sound system and a view of the lovely gardens through the conservatory windows. Harriet Larsen sat alone in one of the chairs by the window, an untouched cup of coffee steaming beside her on the table. She was looking out the window but Kate would have sworn she saw nothing of the beauty there.

She greeted Kate with a ghost of a smile and a colourless 'hello'.

"How's your sister?" asked Kate, sitting down opposite Harriet.

Harriet shrugged. "She's holding on. There's no change... she's not better but she's not worse. The kids wanted me to take them to see her yesterday but... I didn't think it was right, they would have been so distressed..." She trailed off, her blank gaze returning to the garden.

"Are the children still at school?"

"No, they're with Jack's parents. I don't know whether that's the best thing - they're all so distressed - I don't know, maybe it's good that they can all be together? They were always close to their grandparents—"

Harriet's voice shook into silence. She put a hand up to her face, pinching either side of her nose. "I don't know what to do," she said after a moment and Kate heard simple bewilderment in her tone.

Did they ever think, these perpetrators, of the utter devastation their actions left behind? Did they ever think about the people left to pick up the pieces? Of course they don't, Kate, you idiot, she chided herself. The surge of anger she felt was welcome, it was that which propelled her to become a detective in the first place.

She brought herself back to the task in hand. "Can I get you some more coffee, Harriet?" she asked, seeing that the cup already on the table had cooled.

Harriet shook her head. "No, thanks. I can't seem to eat or drink anything at the moment, it just makes me feel ill."

"Of course," said Kate, in a sympathetic tone. "Try and eat something though, won't you? Otherwise you really will get ill."

Harriet gave her another pale smile. "Was there something you wanted?" she asked.

Kate became brusque. "Yes, there is. I need you to tell me about Jack and Madeline. I know it's going to distress you, but I'm afraid it's too important to wait."

Harriet sat up a little in her chair. "What do you mean? Tell you *what* about Jack and Maddy?"

Kate pulled out her notebook. "I need to know about their relationship. Their marriage. Did they get on? Was it a good marriage?"

A small white dent had appeared on either side of Harriet's narrow nose. "A good marriage?" she said, tightly. "What the hell has any of that got to do with this... this awful thing?"

Seeing Harriet bristle, Kate held up a placating hand. "It's background we need," she said. "We need to know everything we can about the - the victims of the crime. Often that's more important than the information we get about the perpetrator. Do you understand?"

Harriet still had that pinched look of fury on her face. "No. No I don't understand. I don't know why you need to know all the gory details of someone's private business when it's perfectly obvious that this is someone who's come from outside the house, a stranger, some psychopath. What the hell does it matter whether Jack and Maddy got on? Why does that make any difference at all?"

"So, they didn't get on, then?" asked Kate.

"I didn't say that!"

"You mentioned 'gory details'. Where there any?"

"I didn't say anything of the kind," snapped Harriet. She pushed her chair back, preparing to get up.

"Harriet," Kate said, in a tone that was such that the other woman froze in a half crouch. "Please sit down."

Slowly, glaring at Kate, Harriet lowered herself back into her chair.

"Now," said Kate calmly. "I know you're upset. I know you're functioning under an enormous amount of stress. I can sympathise with that. But the longer you push me away and storm off in high dudgeon, the further and further away we get from catching whoever attacked your sister. Who *killed* your brother-in-law. I'm assuming you don't want that, no matter how much you don't want us digging into your sister's marriage and relationships."

Harriet remained silent for a moment, sitting rigidly upright. Then she blew out her cheeks and slumped back into the chair. Tears ran from the corners of her eyes. Kate guessed that their confrontation had just drained what little emotional energy Harriet had had left and while she felt for her, she was glad that the severity of the situation had been recognised.

After a moment, Harriet wiped her face and sat up again. She leant forward and took a sip of the cold coffee, grimacing. "There's not that much to tell," she said, in a low voice. "Nothing too scandalous, I mean. The weird thing is that Jack and Maddy were always a bit of an odd couple. Jack was always so clever, I mean really intellectual and Maddy - well, she wasn't stupid, not at all, but academia was never her thing. She was always more about having fun, if you see what I mean, although don't get me wrong, she's no ditsy airhead, not at all."

"They met at university?"

"Yes. I'm sure I mentioned that before. Anyway, they got together at uni and stayed together. Got married in... when was it? 2002 and had Alicia a year later. Harry was born in... um... 2005."

Kate was busy scribbling. "Would you say it was a happy marriage?" she asked, looking up to gauge Harriet's reaction. The other woman half smiled.

"Yes. Yes, it was. It wasn't perfect, of course. What marriage is?"

"Well," said Kate, "I'm sure you're right."

There was a minute of silence broken only by the scratching of Kate's pen on her notepad. Then she looked up. "And?"

Harriet looked at her, warily. "What do you mean?"

"I said, 'and'? What are you keeping back?"

"What—"

"All you've told me is that Jack and Madeline had a good, uneventful, happy marriage. If that's the case, why get so defensive with me when I start asking about it?"

"I – I didn't—"

Kate raised an eyebrow and Harriet collapsed back into her chair again, throwing up her hands. "All right," she almost shouted. Then she sat forward, propping her forehead on her hands. "Jack – he – last summer—" She took a deep breath and said "Last summer, they did go through a bit of a rough patch. Okay?"

She clammed up and Kate raised her eyebrows again. "You'll have to be a bit more specific, Harriet."

Harriet bit her lip but the anger had gone out of her face. She looked sad. "All right. Jack – he had an affair. Last summer."

"Can you tell me anything more than that?"

Harriet pushed her hair back from her face. "I don't think it went on for long. Maybe a couple of months. Maddy – she knew something was up for a while before she found out, but she just thought Jack was really stressed out, about the business."

"So, she did find out?"

"He told her. Apparently he and his lady friend decided that they couldn't live with themselves, broke it off and then Jack told Maddy." Harriet's tone was scathing. "Why he couldn't keep it to himself and spare her the pain, I don't know."

"Perhaps he wanted to make a fresh start?"

Harriet snorted. "Yes, maybe. Or maybe he knew he'd get found out eventually and thought he'd better make sure she heard it from him, rather than from anyone else?"

"Like whom?"

Harriet sat back again. "I don't know. I'm just thinking aloud, really."

"Who did Jack have the affair with?"

Harriet had a lock of hair between her fingers and was twirling it between her finger tips, as if examining it for split ends. Displacement activity – Kate did the same when under pressure.

"Someone he worked with," said Harriet. Then she snorted again. "Of course. Not his secretary, or anything like that. I have to say that Jack wouldn't be that clichéd. It was one of the other scientists, Sarah someone."

"Sarah Brennan?"

Harriet's eyes narrowed. "I think so, yes. I don't remember her surname." She paused for a moment and then said in a rush, "Maddy was, well, *incredulous* when she found out. It wasn't like Jack, he was never a Jack the Lad or anything like that." She smiled faintly. "Jack wasn't a Jack the Lad. He never seemed that interested in women."

"But you've only ever known him as your sister's boyfriend and husband, right?"

Harriet sighed. "Yes. Yes, I suppose so."

Kate flexed her aching hand. "So you were surprised, too? Did Madeline confide in you?"

Harriet nodded unhappily. "She'd been telling me something was wrong for a while. Not that she knew what it was, but... she just had a feeling something was wrong."

"So, what happened when Madeline found out?"

Harriet blew out her cheeks and slumped back into her chair again. "She went crazy. Screamed and threw things. Broke a lot of very expensive ornaments. Could you blame her?"

Kate nodded. She paused for a second because she wasn't sure how she could tactfully ask the question she needed to.

"Did Madeline...um... did she take her anger out on Jack?"

Harriet raised an eyebrow. "Yes. Who else? That Sarah woman?"

"No, I mean... did she express it physically?" Kate sighed inwardly and stopped beating around the bush. "Did she attack him, try to hurt him?"

"I doubt it. Well, she might have thrown something at him—" The penny dropped and Harriet sat bolt upright in her chair. "What are you implying? You can't – you can't think that Madeline did this? You can't think that, you can't!"

People at neighbouring tables were beginning to glance over. Kate raised a soothing hand. "I'm not implying anything, Harriet, certainly not what you seem to think I am. I'm just trying to get the bigger picture, that's all."

"You must be crazy if you think that," said Harriet. Angry tears shone in her eyes. "I'd laugh if it wasn't so – so bloody *tragic*. How dare you?"

Kate soothed and murmured and adopted the least aggressive body posture that she could. For all her outrage and overemphasis, she could see that Harriet was genuinely flabbergasted at the prospect of her sister being thought a suspect. Which, despite their marital difficulties, meant it hadn't even occurred to her. That was interesting.

Once Harriet had calmed down a little, Kate decided on a new tactic. "You've told me about Madeline's reaction to Jack's affair. How do you think Jack felt about it?"

"What do you mean?" Harriet took another sip of her cold coffee and almost gagged. "What do you mean, how did Jack feel about it?"

"You've said that he told his wife that he ended the affair. What reason did he give for doing that?"

Harriet shrugged. "Maddy said he said he knew it wouldn't work. He didn't want to lose his children and he didn't think Maddy deserved to be a single mum."

"So he was basically renouncing his affair for them?" Kate scribbled down notes to hide her thoughts. That sounded suspiciously noble to her. What if there was another reason? Did Jack Dorsey just not fancy what would no doubt be a whopping divorce settlement if the marriage had broken up? But then, why take the risk of telling your wife, if that were the case?

Harriet had gone back to staring out of the window. "I suppose so," she said, after a moment.

Kate tapped her pencil on her pad. "Did they ever split up, after Jack came clean?" she asked. "Did he ever move out, for example?"

Harriet shook her head. "No. No, that never happened. I suppose after a while it just got – got swept under the carpet."

Kate made a noise of assent. There were still so many questions she wanted to ask but, before she antagonised Harriet any further, she wanted to run a few things past Anderton first. And she knew who else she needed to talk to as a matter of priority. Sarah Brennan.

Chapter Thirteen

KATE HAD ARRANGED TO MEET Sarah Brennan at her home. It was a conversation that was probably better conducted in private, although Kate had been careful not to give any hint of what she wanted to talk to Sarah about when they made the arrangement. Sarah probably thought Kate wanted to talk to her to find out more about Michael Frank. Kate thought about Michael as she drove to Sarah Brennan's house. Were they coming at this from entirely the wrong angle? Could Michael Frank's death really be unconnected with the murder of Jack Dorsey? Was it just horrible coincidence? No, I can't accept that, Kate thought as she found a parking space. She checked her hair was smooth, pulled the shoulders of her jacket straight and got out of the car.

Sarah Brennan lived in a nondescript semi-detached house, built sometime in the nineteen fifties. It wasn't an attractive house but it was well maintained, the small front garden neat, if not particularly interesting to look at; merely a square of well-cut lawn and some shrubs around the borders. The front door was one of those unattractive plastic ones. Kate rang the doorbell and waited. She realised she had absolutely no idea what a scientist like Sarah earned for a living. Presumably working in the private sector, rather than the National Health Service, would be slightly more lucrative...?

Kate had met Sarah before and was therefore, slightly ridiculously, expecting her to be dressed in her usual white lab coat. Of course, at home, Sarah wore casual clothes; jeans, a plain blue T-shirt. She wore no makeup and her dark and plentiful hair was loose around her face. As she made coffee for herself and Kate in the open-plan kitchen and dining area, Kate observed her. Sarah must have been in her late forties, perhaps early fifties. She was slightly overweight, but in an attractive way, with a clearly defined waist, heavy hips and a large bust. Kate thought back to the photograph she'd seen of Madeline Dorsey; blonde, petite, slim and sexy. Why had Jack jettisoned his ostensibly more desirable wife for this no doubt clever but much more homely woman? Kate gave herself a sharp mental slap for thinking such sexist thoughts, but it was true, wasn't it? Why had he done it?

The coffee that Sarah gave her was good, hot and strong. The other woman sat down at the pine kitchen table, opposite Kate. She had shown no sign of emotion, anxiety or upset as yet; the soft edges of her face were placid in repose. There was a kind of restful quality about her, Kate noticed; she gave the impression that she would rarely be hurried, or upset. Was that what had attracted Jack Dorsey?

Kate swallowed her mouthful of coffee and began. "Thanks very much for seeing me, Sarah. I'd like to talk to you about Jack Dorsey."

Sarah's face flickered for a moment but the movement was soon gone. "Oh yes?" she said, a trifle coolly.

Kate took a deep breath. "You and he had quite a long affair, didn't you?"

The histrionics that such an accusation would normally invoke in a suspect weren't forthcoming. Sarah's well-shaped eyebrows twitched upwards for a moment. "Who on Earth told you that?" she asked, in a fairly normal tone.

"Harriet Larsen."

"I don't know who that is, sorry."

"She's Madeline Dorsey's sister."

The calmness flickered again. Sarah's eyes met Kate's and then looked away.

"I see," was all that she said, after a short silence.

"Is it true?"

Sarah placed her empty cup back on its saucer and the chime of china against china rang out into the room. "Oh, yes, it's true," she said.

"Can you tell me—" Kate began and then stopped

as Sarah's face suddenly crumpled and collapsed inwards. The other woman began to cry, silently at first and then with harsh, tearing sobs. After a minute, she put her head on the table, hiding her face from Kate with shaking hands.

Kate waited. After an uncomfortably long time, Sarah Brennan's crying tapered off. Eventually, there was nothing left of the storm of emotion but the occasional gasping hitch in her breathing.

Sarah sat up slowly. "I'm sorry," she said. Her voice was steadier than Kate had expected. Sarah looked at her with wet eyes. "I loved him, you see," she said simply.

Kate nodded. She fished a clean tissue from her bag and held it out to Sarah.

"Thanks." There was a pause while she mopped her face and blew her nose. "It was wrong, of course it was. He was married with children. That's why it had to end."

"Really?" said Kate, trying to keep the cynicism from her voice.

Sarah half smiled, not fooled. "I know, it sounds ridiculous. But the thing about Jack—" Her voice shook and she cleared her throat. "The thing about Jack was that he had integrity. I know that sounds stupid, given he was cheating on his wife. But, he really did have integrity. And morals. That's why we – our relationship – couldn't carry on. It was tearing

158

him apart. And he couldn't stand the thought of not living with his children."

Kate clamped down on what she wanted to say, which was if Jack Dorsey was so concerned about day to day life with his children, why the hell had he sent them away to boarding school?

"How did your affair start?" was what she asked instead.

Sarah looked away, towards the kitchen window. "It was about a year ago." Her gaze was far away, obviously remembering. "It was one of the new formulas, we were working on it together." She transferred her gaze from the window to Kate. "We understood each other. We worked well together."

Kate raised her eyebrows encouragingly and Sarah went on.

"He didn't talk much about his marriage. He and Madeline had met at university and I think – well, I think when he met her he was a bit bowled over that someone like her would go for someone like him. You know. Jack was wonderful but he wasn't – he wasn't glamorous. Not like Madeline."

"Do you think they had a happy marriage?"

Sarah's gaze fell. "I don't know. But - he was lonely. I know he was lonely. I'm lonely myself, sometimes – who isn't?" Her steady brown gaze met Kate's and Kate was unable to look away this time. "We're all lonely sometimes, aren't we? But I tell you, being lonely in a marriage is worse, I think.

You're there in life with someone who's supposed to understand you and be with you, and when you don't have that, well, it's a terrible thing really, isn't it?"

"You and Jack talked a lot about work, I presume?"

Sarah half smiled again. "That's right. We're both – we were both passionate about our work. Jack liked to have someone to talk to about it. He doesn't get that – I mean, he didn't get that with Madeline. Even with Alex. Alex is very clever, of course, but I always get the impression that the important thing for him is the money, not the science itself." She was screwing the damp tissue into a ball in her hand. "Actually, it's funny... that's reminded me..." She tailed off.

"Yes?" Kate prompted, after a moment.

"Nothing. It's nothing. It's just that Jack said something about money, once. I know he was worried about it. I just can't remember exactly what he said..."

"Jack Dorsey was worried about money?"

Sarah transferred the tissue ball from one hand to the other. "I don't know, I can't remember. We didn't always talk..."

She smiled a smile that held all kinds of secrets. It was gone in a flash and a heavy look of sadness settled back over her face. Kate tried pushing her for more details on what she'd just mentioned, but

Sarah insisted that she couldn't remember anything more. "It was just a throwaway remark. I can't remember any more. I'm sorry."

Kate nodded. There was a short silence before Kate broke it. "I may need to talk to you again, Sarah. If I give you my card, can you call me or contact me if you remember anything else that you think might be important?"

Sarah nodded. "Are you any further with the investigation into Michael's death?"

Kate looked up from closing her handbag after extracting one of her business cards. "Michael Frank? We're following up several leads. That's about all I can say at the moment."

Sarah nodded again. "He was an amazing man, too. I always had a bit – God, this sounds awful telling you now when you know about Jack." She coloured and cleared her throat. "I always had a soft spot for Michael. Nothing happened. He wasn't interested in me, not like that. But... oh, it's hopeless, isn't it?" She didn't appear to expect an answer. "The good die young, don't they? That's what they say."

Tears were forming in her eyes. She didn't see Kate to the door, but remained at the kitchen table, looking off into space again. Kate let herself out, closing the horrible plastic door behind her softly.

Chapter Fourteen

"WELL, THAT'S INTERESTING."

Anderton paced up and down the office floor. Kate, momentarily distracted, wondered whether he'd actually wear a path in the laminate, one day. She dragged her attention back to what he was saying.

"Let me recap, Kate. You're saying that Sarah Brennan had a fairly lengthy affair with Jack Dorsey and you're also telling me that she had a thing for Michael Frank."

"Well, that's what she said." Kate brushed her hair out of her eyes. "She also told me that Jack Dorsey was worried about money, or said something of the kind."

Anderton rubbed his chin. "Sarah Brennan, sexually involved with Jack Dorsey, who is now dead. Sarah Brennan, apparently emotionally involved with Michael Frank, who is also dead. Could it be—" He didn't finish, but started pacing again. The others watched him.

SNARL

"Oh, this is insane," Anderton said, stopping suddenly. "It can't possibly be her. Could it?"

Olbeck shook his head. "Her alibi checks out for both deaths. And why would she kill Dorsey so savagely, anyway? She said she loved him."

"'Hell hath no fury...'" Anderton said absently. He rubbed his chin and looked at the crime scene pictures. "But no, I agree with you. It doesn't make much sense. But, you know, I would swear that there's a woman involved here, somewhere. I can't say why, I can't quite put my finger on it. There's a sexual motive here, sure as eggs is eggs."

"Why do you say that, sir?" asked Theo, frowning.

"I don't know. I can't say. Call it a feeling?"

"So the terrorism's out, then?" said Kate, trying to keep the impatience from her voice.

"No, I'm not saying that, either."

Kate remembered her first impressions of the Dorsey house, when she and Olbeck had arrived after their near miss with the ambulance. Anderton might think that there was a sexual motive underlying the crime, but Kate wondered whether it might be even more prosaic than that. What had her exact thought been? There's a lot of money here...

"I think I should talk to Sarah Brennan again, see if she can elaborate more. Perhaps she can give us some more on Michael Frank," she suggested.

Theo rocked his chair onto its back legs. "What's

going on with our undercover guy?" he asked. "Has he got anything at all?"

"Now that," said Anderton, "is a good question. He's bringing me up to speed, later today. I'll be able to debrief you on any developments tomorrow. Now, what else? We're still waiting on a lot of the forensics." He paused again, staring intently at the crime scene photographs. "I'm hoping that throws something up. Well, if no one else has anything earthshattering to impart, let's break it up and get on with it."

The team drifted back to their desks. Kate sat down, adjusted her keyboard and rolled her chair back and forth. She felt impatient, not content to do paperwork. She wanted to be out there, questioning, digging, tracking down suspects. She looked across the table at the empty desk opposite. For a moment, she envied Stuart. He wasn't stuck here, in a stuffy office, trawling through reams of data. He was out there in the field; active, a real participant in the hunt.

Olbeck, *en route* to his office, made a detour to come and perch on Kate's desk. "That's just reminded me," he said, gesturing towards Stuart's empty chair. "Stuart's coming round to ours for dinner tomorrow. Fancy joining us?"

"Stuart?" Kate said. "Why?" She realised how rude that sounded and rephrased. "Why are you having him round for dinner?"

"Well, it's not like he can just join us down the pub, is it? And it's lonely work, being undercover. I just thought he might enjoy it, get to know us a bit better, you know. That's why you should come. The more the merrier."

Kate tapped her pen on her jaw, thinking. She felt like hugging Olbeck – he was so *kind*. Always looking out for the underdog, for those on the bottom of the heap. Must be why he likes me so much, she thought gloomily.

"Nothing fancy," said Olbeck. "But Jeff's cooking, so it'll be good. Few beers. You know."

"Who else is going?" asked Kate. She could not help the slight quickening of her pulse at the thought that Anderton might be there.

"Oh, the usual. You, me, Jeff, Stuart, of course. But if you're busy..."

"No, I didn't say that," said Kate, quickly. "I've just got to check with Andrew. I have a feeling we're supposed to be doing something."

When Olbeck had gone back to his office, she reached for her phone and scrolled back through her text messages. Yes, here was the message Andrew had sent about their plans for tomorrow night. Dinner with Kirsten Telling and her husband. Doctor Telling was a pathologist who worked with Andrew; Kate knew her briefly through work and liked her as far as she knew her, but... sitting around a dinner table with two pathologists talking shop wasn't the most appetising social engagement she could think of. She hadn't yet replied to Andrew and did so now. With a quickly suppressed stab of guilt, she declined the invitation. Then she emailed Olbeck. *Am too lazy to walk over, but count me in for tomorrow night. K x.*

STUART ZIPPED UP HIS HOODY and pulled the hood up over his dreadlocks. It was cold for early summer, the blue sky blotted out with threatening grey clouds. As he walked towards the protest table, he was unsurprised to see only two people staffing it and a little cheered to see that they were James and Rosie. Before he could draw near enough to shout hello, he became aware of the angry stance the two of them were taking, squared up to one another, with gesticulating arms and jabbing fingers. Even as he watched, James delivered what was clearly his final hissed remark and stalked off, leaving Rosie behind the stall, flushed and angry, biting her lip.

Stuart's pace slowed to a saunter. He stuck his hands in his pockets, wondering whether to pretend he'd seen nothing or make a suitably tactful remark to Rosie. As he drew level with the table, saying a cautious 'hello', he could see she was close to tears. "You all right?" he asked, throwing discretion to the winds.

Rosie sniffed and swiped her hand across her

cheek. "Oh, I'm fine," she said crossly. "Actually, I'm not fine. You probably saw what just happened."

"Well..."

"James and I had a bit of a row. He's so bloody *stubborn*—" She clamped her mouth together, as if she wanted to say a lot more, turned away and busied herself with tidying the leaflets into a pile.

"Do you need a hand?" Stuart offered.

Rosie exhaled. She shoved a pile of leaflets away from her, put her hands into the small of her back and stretched. "You know what, Mike?" she said. "I'm sick to death of it all. All of it. I have had enough today, I really have."

Stuart's heartbeat picked up a little. The mood she was in, he might be able to get more information that he'd ever managed before. "You know what?" he suggested. "You're right. Let's leave it for today. Come for a drink."

Rosie took her hands away from her back and looked at him in surprise. She had clearly not been expecting him to say that but, after a moment, she lifted her chin and said "Yeah, you're right. I'd love a drink."

"Let's go, then. I'm buying."

They went to the same pub they'd visited on the night they met. Rosie made a beeline for a table at the back while Stuart bought the drinks. When he brought them to the table, she was staring into space, chewing her lower lip.

"Sorry," she said as he sat down. "I'm still angry, I guess."

"Want to tell me about it?"

"There's nothing really to tell... he wants one thing and I want another. Humph." She downed half her pint in three large gulps. Stuart watched her long, smooth throat ripple and reminded himself to keep his mind on the job. Inevitably, his thoughts went to Angie. Three days now, without any contact. It worried him how much he missed her.

"Seen Angie lately?" he asked, before he could stop himself.

Rosie, who'd been in the middle of a monologue about James' shortcomings, looked surprised. Then she frowned. "Why'd you ask?"

"I just wondered. I thought you guys were friends."

"What's James been telling you?"

"Nothing," said Stuart, startled at her tone. "I haven't – I haven't heard anything."

Rosie knocked back the rest of her drink in one go. "Well, we are *friends*," she said, wiping her mouth with a gasp. "But that's it."

"Right," Stuart said. Thinking he'd better change the subject, he asked her what she wanted to drink and went up and bought another round.

After another few pints, Rosie's mood changed

again. Stuart was being as attentive and charming as he could be, pulling out all his best activist anecdotes and making her laugh and shriek with recognition.

"All4One, I remember them. I used to go out with a guy who was with them. He was this mad painter, used to do these huge junk sculptures, like robots made out of cars and things."

"Yeah, I know," said Stuart, nodding. All4One were a radical group, half creative types, half anti-globalisation activists who'd come to national attention when they'd turned a huge empty Hampstead mansion into a commune and art studio before being violently evicted, two months later. "I saw his stuff at Glastonbury, I think," Stuart went on. He tipped his empty pint glass back and forth, in what he knew would be a vain prompt for Rosie to buy her round. "Did you ever live there?"

"At the HQ?"

"The Hampstead place, yeah?"

Rosie shook her head. "No, never lived there. We had a few parties there. Then, I don't know, it all got a bit weird..."

There was a subtle shift in the atmosphere that made Stuart sit up mentally. "Oh yeah?" he asked, careful to keep his tone casual.

Rosie had drunk enough to throw caution to the winds. She propped her chin on one unsteady hand, looking at Stuart intently through her fringe.

"Yeah, weird. When I was there it was all about art and creativity, all that life force stuff – used for good, you know. But then Kitten came and suddenly it was all about—"

She broke off suddenly and went to tip up the last of her fourth pint. Stuart drummed his fingers on his leg under the table, unsure of whether to break the sudden bond that had appeared between them in order to get her another drink. He knew as well as anyone that when you broke up a two-some, it was sometimes impossible to regain that fragile connection.

He stayed put.

"Kitten?" he asked, with just the right amount of curiosity in his voice. He hoped.

Rosie was staring into the depths of her empty glass. She turned it round and round, watching the last few dregs spiral at the bottom of the glass. "Yeah," she said eventually. "He's a bit of a nutter."

"Who is he?"

Rosie shrugged. "One of Angie's friends. Huh, *friends*." She smiled cynically for a moment and Stuart was surprised at the stab of jealousy he experienced as he got her meaning. "He used to be in the army, fought in Iraq. He's really into animal rights; I remember him saying that human beings were the worst things on the planet, once. I think he likes animals a lot more than he likes people. He hates people."

Stuart was listening, holding his breath. He knew he'd heard that strange name before – where had it been? After a moment, it came to him. The party at the squat, James saying with a loaded voice to Angie – 'Seen Kitten lately?' And she'd turned and said coolly, 'Not lately, no...'

Rosie had taken out her phone and was scrolling through her photographs. She held the screen out to Stuart. "Here's HQ. Look at it, isn't it massive? Bloody obscene, something that big belonging to one person."

Stuart looked. There was Angie, sexy in a tight black dress, incongruous against the graffitied wall that stood in the background. She was looking at the camera, the man beside her was looking at her. Again, Stuart felt that jump of jealousy and stamped down hard on it. He looked more closely at the man. Tall, well-built, balding. One muscular arm bore a sleeve of blue and red tattoos.

"Who's that beef-cake?"

Rosie giggled. "That's Kitten."

Under the table, Stuart clenched his fist in a jump of exhilaration. He wondered whether he'd be able to steal Rosie's phone without her knowledge. Probably not...

Stuart made interested noises and Rosie scrolled through a few more photos. The man called Kitten appeared in several more; in one he was smiling at the camera, the maw of a broken or missing tooth visible far back in the right hand side of his mouth, crows-feet around the dark eyes. Dead eyes – there was nothing there, in the depths. Stuart could feel the first prickle of anticipation as he looked at the man in the photograph. He'd seen eyes like that before. You're it, mate, he thought. I've got you.

"Kitten's a weird name for a bloke," he said, still with a casual note in his voice. Rosie was still scrolling through her pictures, chuckling, occasionally shaking her head.

"Yeah, well, it's not the weirdest thing about him by a long shot, take it from me."

"What's his real name?"

"Guy. Guy Something. Guy Ward? Something like that. Don't know, really."

Rosie tapped the screen of her phone. She was casting suggestive glances at her empty pint glass. Stuart knew he should keep questioning her, but he was already late for Anderton. Besides, get her any drunker and she'd be incoherent anyway.

"Listen, Rosie, I've got to go. Got to see someone about a dog."

She smiled lopsidedly at that. He took pity on her and handed her a ten pound note.

"Get yourself another drink. Only one more though, okay? Get yourself a taxi home."

She pouted but took the money. He had a moment's qualm that he was leaving a vulnerable girl to drink by herself in a not-too-salubrious pub.

There was an older woman behind the bar though, and he thought she'd probably keep any eye out. He chucked Rosie under the chin and left, the name running through his head. Guy Ward. Guy Ward. I've got you.

Chapter Fifteen

WHENEVER KATE AND OLBECK GOT together outside of work, they had a kind of informal rule that they didn't talk shop. If Jeff was there, being a polite man who was interested in other people, he'd sometimes ask Kate about her work and she'd happily tell him what she could. But, most of the time, the three of them talked about other things: art and music, films and politics, and funny anecdotes from their past. Kate was unsure of what was going to happen tonight, with Stuart there as well. Would he even be able to talk about the case, given that what he was doing was so secretive?

He was the last to arrive and although he was smartly dressed, in a suit and white shirt, accompanied by a really good bottle of wine, Kate was quite shocked at the look of exhaustion on his face. His eyes were ringed with shadow and his cheeky grin, that had so annoyed her on first meeting him, was nowhere to be seen. It must be tiring, she thought, having to pretend to be someone else all the time. Never able to let your guard down. Not knowing who you could trust. No wonder she'd heard that undercover officers tended to burn out quickly. A few years and they were out of the game. Perhaps that wouldn't be such a great career move for her, after all.

Mark and Jeff were charming hosts and Kate could see Stuart gradually relaxing as he was plied with food and drink, and kind attention. She took a back seat, maintaining a civil silence while the men chatted. She wanted to do full justice to Jeff's excellent cooking, too – Kate really did hope Mark appreciated his good fortune in having a partner who was so skilled in the kitchen. Andrew is too, she reminded herself, dutifully.

After a short period of inattention, Kate came back to the present, realising Stuart was actually addressing her directly. He was asking her about the serial killing case last year, asking her about her injury. She felt a flash of annoyance that, for once, she'd actually managed to forget about that for half an evening, only to be rudely reminded.

"I'm fine now," she told him, trying not to sound too cool.

"It's not easy though, is it?" said Stuart, actually sounding rather humble for a change. "I got shot once. That took years to get over."

"Well, it would, wouldn't it?" said Kate, trying not to let her eyes widen. She struggled for a moment, not wanting to indulge her curiosity – she was sure he was just saying it to show off – and then gave in. "What happened?"

"It was a drug-ring case. Only my second job. Working alongside a lot of bad people and I ran into the wrong one, one night."

"Bloody hell," said Olbeck, topping up Stuart's glass. "Where did you get shot?"

"We were down on the docks—"

"No," said Olbeck, laughing. "Where physically?"

"Oh, right." Stuart smiled, a ghost of his previous grin. Kate assumed that it was a memory that probably wasn't a great deal of fun to recall. "In the chest. Shattered my collarbone on this side." He indicated with his hand. "I was lucky, though. He was going for my heart."

"You must have been out of action for a while," said Kate, thinking of her own long, slow recovery.

Stuart nodded. "I was. It was worth it, though. We smashed the ring. Good job too – these people were scum."

He looked grim, suddenly, truly forbidding. There was a short silence and Jeff got up to clear the plates.

"It's why I joined the force," Stuart said suddenly. He was looking down at the table, his brows drawn together. "My brother was a heroin addict. He died young."

"Oh, I'm sorry," Kate said. She felt a sudden and

genuine surge of sympathy for him. One of her older siblings had died in a car crash at eighteen. Kate had barely known her half-brother, born years before she was, but she still remembered the devastation that his death had caused her family. That was when her mother's drinking had taken a distinct turn for the worse, not that it had ever been very good. Kate hadn't spoken to her mother in almost two years. They were estranged, she supposed, and despite her awful childhood, despite everything, she was swamped by a sudden wave of depression.

She and Stuart were briefly alone at the table as Jeff took plates into the kitchen and Olbeck went to find more wine. Their eyes met and Kate was shocked again by the sudden connection she felt with Stuart – not a sexual feeling, but a brief flicker of emotional closeness. It only lasted a moment, before his gaze dropped away and Olbeck came back with an opened bottle, but the small glow of warmth remained.

They all talked about other things and police work wasn't mentioned again until right at the end of the evening, when Olbeck asked if there was any progress. Stuart nodded. "We've got a name. A name with a history. I expect Anderton will brief you all tomorrow."

"Well, that's great," said Olbeck. He was helping Kate on with her jacket. "Does that mean you're back with us, again?"

Stuart half laughed. "I wish. Not yet. There's still a lot of work to do, so..."

Kate picked up her handbag. "Just as well the boys had you over for dinner tonight, then," she said, smiling. "Sounds like you won't be joining us for after work drinks, any time soon."

"No, that's right. And thanks," said Stuart holding out a hand to Olbeck. Jeff was lounging in the kitchen doorway, a tea towel slung over his shoulder. "Thanks very much, guys. I enjoyed it."

"Our pleasure," said Jeff.

Kate and Stuart left the house together, waving to Olbeck and Jeff, who were framed in the doorway.

"Can I give you a lift?" asked Kate and caught herself, realising that she wasn't even supposed to be seen talking to him in public.

"No, I'm good," Stuart said, absently. "My car's just up here. Listen, Kate..."

He trailed off. Kate waited and then said, "Yes?" in an encouraging way.

"Doesn't matter. Forget I said it. Thanks, Kate, good night."

And with that, he was gone. Kate walked slowly to her own car, pondering. What had that been all about? She got the impression that he'd wanted to confide in her. Was that possible? Confide in her, a virtual stranger, because of that odd little moment of connection they'd experienced? He might have been about to ask you out, she told herself; but that was vanity talking. It wasn't the impression she got. Dismissing her inner musings, she unlocked the car, got in, re-locked the doors and drove away.

YOU FOOL, STUART TOLD HIMSELF as he unlocked his own car. For a second, he'd almost told Kate about Angie; how much he missed her, why he had no idea how she had so strong a hold over him. The words had come surging up his throat and, for a moment, he'd actually thought about saying them. You fool. Why would Kate even be interested, anyway? He liked her, although he got the impression she didn't think much of him. In a funny way, Kate reminded him of his kid sister, Charlotte – Charlie. Physically they weren't much alike, but Kate had that same sort of doughty scrappiness he associated with Charlie – a kind of 'screw you, world, I can take care of myself' type aura that shone out over her neat exterior. It was clear to see that she'd been pretty shaken by that knife incident last year, but that wasn't surprising. Theo had told him the whole story, the second day he'd joined the Abbeyford team, and then when Kate had finally made it back to the office, Stuart could see the vulnerability that lurked under her cool manner. Of course, it was hard getting back on the job, he really did know that.

He drove back to his bedsit slowly, tired after a

long day and somnolent with Jeff's good food. That Mark Olbeck was a lovely guy, too. It was funny, but he'd never had a gay mate before; not that he was homophobic or anything like that, it just hadn't happened. Stuart wondered what it would have been like for Olbeck, declaring his sexuality to the rest of the officers in the station. Pretty nerve-racking, and that was from someone who'd put their life on the line on more than one occasion.

Stuart parked the car, switched off the engine and sat for a moment, rubbing his eyes. He was bushed. He wearily climbed the dank little staircase to his room and opened the door, realising a second too late that it was already ajar. He stopped dead, nerves singing. There was someone in his bed.

A second after the adrenaline kicked in, the bedside light snapped on. It was Angie, resting on one pale arm. He could see she was naked. She said nothing, but looked at him with a heavy-lidded gaze, that incredible face wearing that same indefinable look of challenge that he'd first noticed about her.

"Evening," said Stuart, his tone belying the thudding of his heart. "How did you get in?"

Angie smiled. "Your neighbour was kind enough to help me out."

"My neighbour?" Stuart had barely seen any of the other occupants of the adjoining rooms. And how the hell did his neighbour have a key to his – Stuart's – room?

Angie's smile grew. "Okay, he didn't. I picked the lock. It's only a Yale one – quite simple, really. You really ought to get a stronger one fitted."

"So I can see." Stuart hadn't as yet made any move towards the bed. That faint warning bell was ringing louder this time, like an increasingly loud siren in his mind. *Danger ahead.*

Angie twitched the covers a little and he could see a little more of her. He swallowed. He thought he'd missed her, but up until this moment, with Angie present before him, he hadn't quite realised the depths of his longing. It was visceral.

"Come on, then," said Angie gently, almost maternally. As he stumbled towards the bed, Stuart's last coherent thought was of his dead brother, lost back there in the past. I miss him, he thought, and then Angie's arms were around him and he didn't think of much else for what seemed like a very long time.

Chapter Sixteen

THE SUNLIGHT WOKE HIM, STREAMING through the curtains that didn't quite meet in the middle, lancing through the gap like a spear of molten gold. Stuart lay there quietly, watching the dust motes spin and dance in the beam of light. He was conscious of Angie, breathing quietly beside him. It was the first time they'd slept together, in the literal sense of the word. Perhaps he hadn't so much fallen asleep as much as passed out, exhausted by the long day and by Angie's voracious demands.

Moving quietly, he eased himself out of bed. He'd spotted Angie's handbag over by the chair against the wall. Stamping down on the last remnants of conscience that still remained, even after years of undercover work, he extracted her phone and, keeping a wary eye on her sleeping form, scrolled through the large list of names and numbers stored in the Contacts section. He went straight to the 'Ks' and, despite knowing he'd find it, there was still the drop and twist of his stomach as he saw Kitten's name and a mobile number underneath it. Quickly, he scribbled it down. Angie made a muttering, sighing sound from the bed and Stuart, heart thumping, put the phone back, noting as he did so that the top contact in Angie's phone was a number stored with no corresponding name. He had no time to investigate further – Angie was waking up. He moved swiftly away from her bag, busying himself at the little table where he kept an electric kettle and instant coffee.

"Morning," said Stuart casually, handing her a mug of coffee. He realised he had no idea how she liked it, but guessed she would drink it black with no sugar. She took it from him with no comment but a smile. She sat up in bed quite unselfconsciously to drink it. Stuart tried not to be distracted by the sight of her breasts, something he was still unused to.

Angie drank her coffee in several fast gulps, put the cup to one side, yawned and stretched like a cat.

"I wondered what had happened to you," said Stuart, trying not to sound accusing. Angie smiled.

"I've been busy. I'm working on a big piece at the moment."

"Piece?"

"A new multi-media project. It'll be the best thing I've ever done." She went far away for a moment, her eyes looking at something that Stuart couldn't see. "It's *consumed* me."

Stuart felt embarrassed when she talked like this. It sounded, what? Pretentious. Phony. She believed it, though, and that was somehow more embarrassing than anything else.

"That's good," he said, rather limply.

Angie came back to life. "I can't show you anything yet," she said. She smiled. "Soon you'll be able to see."

"Can't wait," said Stuart, grinning. "Will this be the piece that makes you famous?"

"Oh yes," said Angie, seriously. She cocked her head on one side for a moment. "I can't show you *that* at the moment, but have a look at some of my early work."

Oh God... Stuart pinned an interested look in his face whilst Angie scrambled out of bed and hunted in her bag. He could feel the scrap of paper with Kitten's number on it burning a hole in his pocket.

If he had put the phone back in the wrong place, Angie didn't seem to notice. She retrieved her phone and flung herself back on the bed next to him. He kept that interested look on his face as she scrolled through a variety of photographs. He didn't know much about art – and I don't know what I like, he finished with an inner grin.

Angie's stuff was a mixed bunch; some sculpture, some paintings, an enormous collage that seemed to incorporate a television screen that showed the same loop of film over and over again, a woman riding a bicycle with a large fish in the front basket. Stuart said 'fantastic', 'that's incredible', 'I like what you've done there' and other such inanities. He had the feeling that Angie was barely listening to him anyway; she was absorbed in her pictures.

"This is my last but one project," she said eventually.

"Oh yes?"

"Yes."

She held the screen in front of him. It was another collage, with an integrated screen, but this time, the film shown was – Stuart blinked – a montage of scenes of animal cruelty. A fox disappearing under a yapping flood of beagles. A cow, stun-gunned, its freshly cut throat glistening as the blood pumped away. A blurry shot of someone beating a cow at what looked like a market.

"Far out," he said faintly. He could tell Angie was looking slyly sideways at him, wondering whether he was going to react. "That's... um... powerful."

"It is, isn't it?" said Angie, with satisfaction. "Really makes you look twice. I got some very interesting reactions to that one."

"I'm not surprised."

"That was a commissioned piece."

"Really?" said Stuart, unable to hide the surprise in his voice. Before he could stop himself, he blurted out, "So, people actually *buy* your stuff then?"

A chill settled upon the room. Stuart mentally

kicked himself and tried to make amends. "It's fantastic, though," he said hastily. "Really powerful."

Angie said nothing. She slid her finger across the screen of her phone in one slow, deliberate swipe, hiding the pictures from view.

Stuart knew when to stop. This was a bad time to ask what he had to ask, but he had the feeling that it wouldn't make much difference now, anyway.

"Listen," he said. "I'm trying to get hold of someone and I think you might know them."

"Oh yes?" she said, indifferently. Her features had settled into a beautiful but stony mask.

Stuart swallowed, trying to get some liquid into his dry mouth. "His name's Guy, but everyone calls him Kitten."

The pause was there; infinitesimal, but there. His heart sank. Then Angie said coolly, "Kitten? I haven't seen him in months. What do you want him for?"

It was an innocent enough question, but there was something in her inflection that made Stuart's heart spike again.

"Nothing much," he said, as casually as he could. "I knew him a long time ago, at HQ. Just wanted to catch up with him, if he's around."

"HQ? What's that?"

His heart dipped again. He remembered Rosie's photograph of her, with Kitten by her side.

"Just a place. So, you haven't seen him, or anything? I used to have his number, but I lost it."

Angie got up and started pulling on her clothes, the same white vest and black combat trousers that he'd seen her wear before. "He changes it all the time," she said. There was a tiny mirror hanging by the door and she took a brief, assessing look into it, smoothing her flat cap of hair back into place.

Stuart knew when to not push things. "Thanks for coming over," he said. "Your art is fantastic."

She gave him a brief smile, which he saw in her reflection in the mirror. Then she snatched up her bag and was out the door, closing it behind her in a movement that wasn't quite a slam.

KATE INTERVIEWED SARAH BRENNAN AT the laboratories the next day. Expecting her, Sarah ushered her into a small office that stood off the corridor from the main laboratory and shut the door.

"Parvinder's ears are on stalks," Sarah said, pulling a swivel chair forward for Kate to sit in. "I thought we could probably do with some privacy."

"Yes, indeed." Kate settled herself and began. "Sarah, when we met before, you mentioned something about Jack Dorsey and money – specifically that he was worried about money. Can you tell me anything else about that?"

Sarah hadn't sat down, possibly because there wasn't another chair. She rested against the edge of a desk, her arms folded across her chest. She was composed today, no sign of tears, her voice quiet but firm. "I already said, it was just a throwaway comment. I don't really know what I can tell you. It was just one conversation we had, and not much of anything of significance was said."

"I'll be the judge of that," Kate said, as nicely as she could. She leant forward a little. "What exactly did Jack say?"

Sarah frowned. "I can't remember it word for word."

"Just tell me what you can remember."

Sarah's gaze dropped. "We – we were in bed. Just talking, you know, lying next to one another. Jack went quiet and I – God forgive me, I thought he was thinking of Madeleine – but when I asked, he said something like 'Sorry love, it's just work. There's something not quite right at work.' And of course, I said, 'What do you mean?' thinking he'd run into difficulties with the new formula and I was feeling a bit miffed that he hadn't said anything to me before, you know, professionally. And then he said something like 'No, it's money. Just money stuff.'"

Kate paused in her scribbling. "That's it?"

Sarah shrugged. "That was pretty much it. Oh, and he said something about auditing, or auditors, or something like that."

"He never mentioned this again?"

"No."

"When was this? Can you remember?"

Sarah shifted her position and re-crossed her arms. "I can't be sure, exactly. Since you asked me last, I've been thinking about it and it must have been a few months ago. It wasn't that long ago, I know that."

Kate paused. Something wasn't adding up here. "Sarah," she said slowly. "You told me that your affair with Jack Dorsey finished last autumn. So what were you doing, making pillow talk a few months ago?"

She held Sarah's gaze until the other woman's eyes wavered and dropped.

"Sarah?"

Sarah raised a hand to her face, dropping her head forward. "Things sort of started up again," she said, in what was almost a mumble. "We just – we just couldn't seem to stop ourselves."

"So, tell me exactly, were you and Jack still seeing each other when he died?"

Sarah continued to hide her face and Kate repeated her name sharply. The other woman's head snapped up sharply. Her eyes were brimming with unshed tears. After a moment, she nodded, causing the tears to spill over. She swiped at her own cheeks angrily, wiping them away.

Kate sighed inwardly. "Did Madeline know?"

"I don't think so."

"You don't *think* so? What did Jack say?"

"What do you mean?"

"I mean," said Kate, unable to keep the sarcasm from her voice this time. "Was there going to be another heroic casting aside of his lover for the good of the family? Or did he learn from the last time and decide discretion was the better part of valour?"

Sarah flushed and bit her lip. "He didn't say," she said after a moment.

Kate could see her trying to get angry and decide that it possibly wasn't the brightest thing to do. "What were you doing on the night of Thursday the ninth of May?"

Sarah blinked. "What do you mean?"

"Can you tell me what you were doing on the night of Thursday the ninth of May, specifically between the times of eleven pm and two thirty am?"

Kate knew Sarah's alibi had already been checked, for the times of both the crimes, but she wanted to see what she said. Sarah told her more or less exactly what she'd said before in her statement; she'd visited her elderly mother and stayed the night, the two of them having dinner at home and watching television, before bed at eleven pm. Kate nodded, satisfied. She knew from reading the CCTV reports that Sarah's car had remained outside her mother's address all night.

"I need to talk to Alex Hargreaves," Kate said, getting up. Sarah moved back a little. She was holding herself rigid, her face hard with the effort of appearing composed. "Do you happen to know if he's here?"

Sarah cleared her throat. "He's not, as it happens. He's taking a few days' leave."

"Perhaps you should do the same," said Kate. She said it gently, but the other woman flinched, still raw with revelations. Kate said goodbye quietly and left the office, shutting the door behind her and leaving Sarah Brennan inside, silent and staring off into space.

Chapter Seventeen

"Morning, team," Anderton bellowed, crashing through the door in customary style. "I hope you're all feeling bright-eyed and bushy-tailed this morning, as we have a lot to get through. Wake up, young Theo—" he caught the new DS in a huge yawn. "Late night, was it? Chuh, you young things. Anyway, settle yourselves and let's get started."

Kate sat up keenly. Again, she felt that welcome sense of enthusiasm, of excitement, almost; that things were finally moving and she was part of it.

Anderton indicated a large pile of cardboard folders on his desk. "Right, PM results are back, as well as various forensic reports from the crime scene – the Dorsey crime scene. Take a while to familiarise yourself with what's in them, but I'll summarise for you; Dorsey died of multiple stab wounds, inflicted by a right-handed person. He had defence wounds on both hands and forearms, indicating he was facing his attacker at the time. Darryl Timms, the security guard, died of a single incision to the neck, also from a right handed person. No defence wounds. He was attacked from the side."

"What about Madeline Dorsey?" asked Kate, for the benefit of the team. She and Anderton had already discussed it beforehand.

"The doctors have indicated that there's a possibility that her injuries could be self-inflicted. *Could* be."

There was a brief silence in the room. Anderton gestured to Kate. "Kate also has some information that might be pertinent. Take it away, Kate."

Kate cleared her throat. "Sarah Brennan's affair with Jack Dorsey wasn't over when he was killed. She confirmed to me yesterday that they were still seeing each other."

Theo whistled softly. "So, did his wife find out? Is that what you're saying?"

Anderton hoisted himself onto the edge of his desk. "I'm not saying anything, I'm just putting the facts out there. Madeline Dorsey found out her husband was having an affair in the late summer of last year."

"He told her," Kate broke in.

"Yes, he told her. Now, we have her sister's statement that Madeline reacted very badly to this unwelcome news. And what's more interesting, is that there didn't seem to be any sort of long-term fallout from Dorsey's revelation. By that, I mean there wasn't any divorce, or talk of divorce, or

Dorsey moving out, or anything like that, that we know of."

Jane raised a hand. "Could that be because Madeline Dorsey was afraid of losing her husband? Might she have just turned a blind eye or told herself that it didn't matter because now it was over?"

Anderton nodded. "Could be. God, I wish that woman would get better, we'd have all the answers we need, then... " Kate raised a censorious eyebrow at his apparent callousness and he caught her eye and grinned. "Of course, we hope she recovers for her own sake, as well. Happy, Kate?"

Kate half-smiled. "Sir, can I just clarify something?" she asked. Anderton nodded. "Am I right in thinking that you're inferring that if Madeline Dorsey found out that her husband was having an affair again that... well, she could have – might have – reacted violently?"

"It's possible," said Anderton. "In an infinite universe, everything is possible."

Olbeck was shaking his head. "I'm not buying it," he said. "Attack her husband, okay, maybe. But to then kill the security guard at the same time? It doesn't make sense. The timing's all wrong. Darryl Timms died *first*, according to the reports. I just cannot see a nice, middle-class mother of two cold-bloodedly deciding to murder her husband and getting rid of the only possible witness first." He strode up to the photograph of Timms' body and pointed. "Look, look at that incision. That's almost, well, professional."

"Exactly," said Anderton. "We are still mired in confusion here. We've got motive for Madeline Dorsey, but there's too many conflicting factors for us to comfortably be able to point to her as our prime suspect. And you're forgetting something else."

Everyone looked at him expectantly. He jumped off the desk and joined Olbeck at the whiteboards, tapping another crime scene photograph. "What about that?"

His finger rested on the photograph of the word written on the wall of the Dorsey's drawing room in blood. *Killer*.

"A bluff?" suggested Rav, tentatively.

"Mmm... possibly." Anderton didn't look convinced. "If we accept Madeline Dorsey is the killer, then surely that means the bombing of Michael Frank's car is actually unrelated to this crime. Does that sound likely to you all?"

There was another silence.

"Anyway," said Anderton, as they all stayed close-mouthed. "I've got something else for you, on that. We have a name from our man in the field."

He held up a print out, an arrest report with the usual mug shot in the top left corner.

"Guy Wade, AKA Gerry Ward, AKA 'Kitten'. He's an ex-soldier, served in Iraq and Afghanistan.

Dishonourably discharged from the army in 2010. Has been arrested numerous times for violence at demonstrations. Strong links with the Animal Liberation Front. Most definitely someone we want pulled in for interview, under caution if necessary. Now, we just have to find the bugger."

There was a noticeable stir of excitement in the room. Anderton smiled, conscious of it. "All right, team. Top priority – find Guy Wade and bring him in. I want Sarah Brennan to make another statement. If anyone else has anything to add, let me know. Got it?"

There was a flurry of nods.

"Great," said Anderton. "Off you go, then."

The room hummed with that concentrated, silent busyness of a group of people intent and focused on their roles. Kate took the print out on Guy Wade and began to scour the multiple entries documenting his arrests and cautions on the relevant databases. At last, she felt like she was actually doing something positive. She found a name and address that she knew would be useful and tapped keys to print out the details, muttering "Yes, yes, yes," under her breath.

She looked up as someone paused by her desk.

"Got a last known address," said Theo, waving a sheet of paper in front of Kate's nose. She batted it away.

"Fine, I'll top that with the army contact who

headed the regiment that Wade used to be belong to."

"We'll do mine first, right?"

Kate sighed inwardly. "If we must."

"Come on, let's go, then." Theo was almost bouncing on his feet. Despite herself, Kate was amused.

"I'm driving," Theo warned.

Kate sighed. "Of course you are."

She waved at Olbeck as they left the office, squashing down the wish that he were coming with her, rather than Theo. As well as being a cocky little so-and-so, Theo liked to listen to rap and RnB as he drove, which gave Kate a headache. Would it be rude, she wondered, to wear her iPod on the journey?

The traffic was fairly heavy on the way out of Abbeyford – the council were engaged in their seemingly interminable plan of digging up every available road to cause maximum inconvenience to all with the resulting roadworks. Theo said as much to Kate, except in words that were somewhat shorter and rather more Anglo Saxon in tone.

"Yes, I know," said Kate. The car inched forward another foot. "Where are we actually going?"

"Swindon. The landlady of the flat that Wade used to rent lives there. He skipped out owing a few months' rent, apparently."

Kate was flicking through the file they'd already

amassed on Guy Wade. "This guy has a serious arrest record. GBH, ABH, civil disorder, resisting arrest..."

"Yeah," said Theo, finally pulling onto the motorway. "I know. Person of Interest, yeah?"

"Mmm." Kate watched the green banks of the motorway roll past. If Wade was the man they were seeking, they needed to find some hard evidence to link him to both or either crime. Just being a criminally violent thug wouldn't be enough, unfortunately.

Chapter Eighteen

THE HOUSE WHERE THEIR SUSPECT used to live was in the middle of a tired estate of mid-century houses, most of which had probably been built as social housing after the Second World War. Here and there were pretty front gardens and a brave – and in the context, somewhat pathetic – attempt to smarten up the exterior of a house. These few well-kept houses stood out in contrast to the dirty pebbledash, broken windows and rubbish-filled front gardens of most of the others. Kate had grown up on an estate not too dissimilar. She felt the same wave of depression wash over her as she had when she used to visit her mother. At least their estrangement meant she didn't have to do that anymore. Silver linings, and all that...

The landlady, Mrs Grenson, was a fat, blousy woman, with greying blonde hair scraped back into a scrappy ponytail and a lit cigarette dangling permanently from her fingers. The building in which she lived had once been a three bedroom house; she now occupied the ground floor, renting out the rooms upstairs as bedsits. Guy Ward had apparently lived there for six months, before disappearing eight weeks earlier.

"What was he like?" asked Kate, trying not to breathe in any more smoke than she had to, a hopeless task.

Mrs Grenson shrugged. "He was quiet, I'll give him that. Didn't make much trouble. Only thing I had to take him up on was the pets. I said no pets, see, and he still brought them in. A kitten and an effing great rabbit. Made a right mess of the carpet, chewed it all up."

"Did he ever have any visitors, people to stay?"

"Not that I ever saw."

"Do you know if he had any family?"

"Nah."

"I don't suppose he left any forwarding address or anything like that?"

Mrs Grenson laughed a cynical laugh. "Nah," she said, again.

"Do you have any tenants now?" asked Theo, as Kate was overtaken by a coughing fit. Mrs Grenson looked at her in disgust, as if she were putting it on.

"Just one. 'E's up there now, if you want to talk to 'im. Number one."

They escaped the downstairs flat thoughtfully and climbed the stairs. The smell of smoke gradually lessened, but was replaced by others just as unpleasant. Kate took a quick look into the bathroom and wished she hadn't.

The tenant of room number one took a long time to answer the door. When he did so, he looked at the police in sleepy confusion, which swiftly became panic as he realised who they were. Noting his bloodshot eyes and the reek of marijuana smoke that came from the room, Kate raised her hand in a placating gesture. "We're not going to arrest you for having a spliff," she said. "So you can calm down. We need to talk to you about Guy Wade."

The tenant, who turned out to be called Paul, looked to be about twenty two; he was skinny and pale, like someone who hadn't seen much daylight recently. He claimed firstly not to know who they were talking about, but after being shown Wade's photograph, foggy comprehension dawned.

"Oh, *that* guy. He was a nutter. Seriously weird eyes, like, I dunno, *dead* or something."

"Were you friends? Did you spend any time with him?"

"That guy didn't have any friends, I'm telling you. No one ever came to see him. He just used to spend his time watching these well loud films or porn. I'm telling you."

"How do you know?"

"These flats are so shit, you can hear everything through the walls, man."

"Did you ever hear him talk on the phone, perhaps?"

Paul sniffed. "Dunno. Oh yeah, maybe a couple of times. He was mumbling though, couldn't really hear what he was saying."

They persisted for a few more questions, but it was obvious that neither Paul nor Mrs Grenson could help them any further. Returning to the car, Kate sniffed her shirt sleeve, grimacing.

"Come on," said Theo, "That wasn't the worst house you've ever been in, not by a long shot."

Momentarily, the bloodied drawing room of the Dorseys' house recurred to Kate.

"No," she said, after a moment. "There have been worse."

Their next destination was Royal Wootten Bassett, the scene of so many sad homecomings of soldiers who'd paid the ultimate price for the service of their country. As Theo drove along the main street, Kate remembered the crowds who turned out to line the pavements, the solemn onlookers, the tearstained faces of the grieving families. Had Guy Wade's experiences in the army turned him from patriot to misanthropist, or did his apparent hatred of the human race go deeper than that?

Guy Wade's once commanding officer, Peter Wentworth, was a distinguished looking man of about fifty, still with a thick head of hair scarcely touched by grey, except at the temples. He reminded Kate a little of Anderton, except without the latter's unceasing energy. Captain Wentworth had a clipped but calm manner, and courteously offered them both refreshments before they got down to business.

"Guy Thomas Wade," said the captain. "Yes, I remember him. He was a troubled man."

"Really?"

"He came from a very lowly background. Born the wrong side of the blanket, no real father figure. Rackety kind of childhood. I only know this second-hand, of course, from his fellow soldiers."

Kate tried not to resent the words used. She'd been 'born on the wrong side of the blanket', stupid term. She'd had a rackety kind of childhood. *We can't all have a privileged upbringing, mate.*

The captain went on speaking. "I often see it in the ranks," he said. "Plenty of men and women join the forces because they're looking for order and stability, and the comfort of having someone else tell you what to do."

Again, Kate was pierced by his words. It was true. Why else had she wanted to be a police officer? Catching the bad guys, of course, that was the conscious reason. But the unconscious one was to bring more order to the chaos of life. She remembered her first week at Hendon, settling in with her dorm-mates. She even remembered the first night there; lying in a strange bed in a strange room, in a building filled with strangers. She should have been homesick – instead, she remembered feeling an overwhelming relief. She remembered Stuart at Olbeck's dinner table, head down, clutching his glass. *That's why I joined the force...*

She brought herself back to the present with an effort. Theo had obviously just asked a question and the captain was frowning.

"There were – incidents," he said. "There were several fights, both with other soldiers and with civilians. It culminated, as you know doubt know, in a discharge from the services."

Kate recalled the notes of the case. "He was involved in the serious beating of an Iraqi citizen, who later died from his injuries," she said. "So, he was court-martialled?"

Captain Wentworth looked uncomfortable. "No. No, it never actually came to that. There was a lack of evidence – one of the key witnesses' testimony was very unreliable. The family of the victim eventually dropped the charges."

"Why?"

Captain Wentworth sat back in his chair, one thumb running along the edge of his jaw. "Let's just say that they probably didn't want too much close attention paid to their... situation. The victim was – well, let's just say he was a person of interest to our side."

Theo looked puzzled. Kate felt like giving him a poke in the ribs.

"They were insurgents?" she asked and watched Theo's face clear.

"Possibly."

"Was it—" Kate looked down at the notes on her lap. "What was Guy Wade's motive for the attack? Did he have one?"

Incredibly, Captain Wentworth chuckled, a single dry cough of a laugh. Then he cleared his throat. "Forgive me. I actually remember what Wade said, after we'd arrested him. He said he did it because the victim had been flogging his donkey."

For a moment, Kate thought that was some kind of sexual euphemism. Then she realised it was the literal truth. Guy Wade had killed a man for being cruel to an animal. She and Theo exchanged a glance.

"One more thing, captain. Did Wade ever work in bomb disposal, or with explosives in any way?"

"No. No, not that I'm aware. We do, of course, have such units in each of our battalions, and it's possible that Wade had some friends or contacts in those units. He was a fairly quick learner. He was a violent, troubled man, like I said, but he wasn't without intelligence."

"SO, WHAT DO YOU THINK?" Kate asked as they made their way back to the car.

Theo glanced over at her. "Sounds like our guy, doesn't it?"

"Yes, it does. So now we just have to find him."

206

Chapter Nineteen

THOSE WERE ANDERTON'S SENTIMENTS WHEN they arrived back at the station for the debrief.

"I need Stuart back here," he said. "Things are moving quickly, now. Someone go and get him in – pretend to arrest him, if you have to."

There were a few grins at this and Kate could see that several people quite fancied the novelty of 'arresting' one of their colleagues. Let's hope we never have to do it for real, she thought.

"Anyone got anything else to add?"

Something had been nagging at Kate, something to do with the whiteboards. As she swept her gaze along them, it snagged on whatever had been nudging her. Someone, Anderton probably, had drawn a couple of pound signs and circled them, right by the crime scene pictures of the Dorsey house. She raised her hand.

"Sir, I'd like to go and interview Alexander Hargreaves. I've got several questions for him."

"Fine. Do that. Take someone with you."

"I'm fine—"

"No buts, DS Redman." Kate fought down an angry blush. Patronising git. "I'm not having my officers wandering around that isolated spot without back-up."

"I'll come," said Theo, helpfully. Kate tried to look grateful.

At least this time Kate could insist on driving, as she'd been there once before and Theo hadn't. Her radio station had been tuned to Classic FM, which came on automatically when she started the engine but she turned it off rather pointedly.

"Cor," Theo said as they drew up beside the lakeside house. "Nice gaff. I'd love something like this."

Kate made an agreeing noise as she parked the car. Theo was craning to see out of the windows, shielding his eyes against the glare of the sunlight.

"I think I saw this on *Grand Designs*, once. I love that show. I'm going to have a place like this, one day."

"Really?" asked Kate, trying not to sound too surprised – or too cynical. She thought of pointing out to Theo that even if he rose to become Chief Superintendent, the likelihood of him being able to afford a multi-million pound house was nothing but a faint, distant dream; but why stamp on the poor bloke's aspirations?

Once they were out of the car, Kate once

again became aware of the sense of isolation. It was a warmer, sunnier day than the time she and Anderton had visited, but there was still a pressing sense of solitude as they stood in the driveway. She could hear the faint lap of the lake waters against the posts of the jetty. The pine trees stood by the lakeside like needled sentinels. A car that Kate vaguely recognised as the large BMW that had been parked here on their previous visit was parked inside the open garage.

"Looks like he's home," she said, and Theo nodded.

But no one answered their knocks on the door and rings of the doorbell. After five minutes, Kate gestured to Theo and they began to walk around the decking that ran along the back of the house. Theo exclaimed over the view.

"I know, it's nice but—" Kate began and then stopped dead.

The long wall of glass at the back of the house was currently in shadow, and the interior of the house was clearly visible. Kate's heart leapt into her throat. Within the dim interior, she could see a figure, slumped in one of the armchairs around the glass coffee table, and there was a dark stain on the fluffy white rug on the slate floor. She clutched Theo's arm.

"Oh, fuck," said Theo, taking it in. "Shit. Is it him?"

"Alex Hargreaves? I think so." Kate pressed her hands up against the glass, trying to see as much as she could through the twin barriers of glass and low light. "Oh my god. Theo, we've got to get in."

"I know." Theo sounded as shaken as she was. She knew what he was thinking – was this another murder? "I'm going to call it in right now, and then we'll get that door down."

They ran back around to the front of the house, Theo already talking to Dispatch. After he'd hung up, he tried Anderton, terminating the call with a curse when he obviously got his voicemail. Kate was already calling Olbeck.

"Oh, Lord," said Olbeck. Kate pressed the phone to her ear, grimacing – he sounded like he was walking down a wind tunnel. "I'm just leaving the office – I'll be there as quick as I can. Are you okay?"

"Fine, we're fine. Just worried about what we're going to find."

"Maybe you should wait 'til the patrol get there."

"We'll be fine," said Kate, trying to keep the impatience from her voice. "Can you get hold of Anderton?"

"He's with the Chief. I'll grab him as soon as he's done."

Kate didn't have faith that the two of them would be able to break the front door down, despite Theo's youth and strength. If he'd had any sense at all, Hargreaves would have built himself an impregnable fortress. But, primed with adrenaline, it only took three shoulder charges before the frame splintered and a gap appeared. Theo kicked the door fully open in just thirty seconds.

Kate braced herself for the peal of an alarm, but there was nothing. After the splintering and crashing of the door break, the silence rolled back in. Kate found herself holding her breath. She was a little ashamed that she let Theo go in first, although he would have probably stopped her if she'd tried to be the one to take the lead. As it was, he held out a protective arm as she stepped forward, which she found simultaneously touching and annoying.

As they stepped over the threshold, Kate was assailed with fear. *This was stupid, we're not armed, we have no idea who might be here...* Over their quick, high breathing, she caught the faint sound of sirens and relaxed a little. Theo edged forward, Kate following him closely, until they were standing in the huge, atrium-like space in the centre of the house.

As soon as she saw the body, Kate felt her fear dissipate. Alex Hargreaves sat in one of the leather chairs, his head rolled forward onto his chest, his eyes closed. Both arms were loose at his sides, the sleeves of his white shirt rolled up to above the elbow. Blood had run from the wounds in his wrists and pooled on the floor beneath him. In front of him, on the glass coffee table, was an empty bottle of whisky, the dregs of which were dried into a sticky amber film in the bottom of a glass. There was a square yellow Post-It note stuck to the glass of the table, with an object placed on top of it. Kate and Theo edged closer. The scrawled writing on the note said the simplest and saddest goodbye of all. *I'm sorry.* The small object was a memory stick. Kate looked closer. Balled-up pieces of pink paper were scattered around Hargreaves' feet and she remembered seeing the same kind of paper bobbing in the lake outside on her previous visit. She leant a little closer, trying to see them in more detail.

"What are those?" she whispered to Theo. It felt wrong to speak in a normal tone.

Theo bent forward to take a closer look. "Not sure," he said after a moment. "Nothing sinister. I think they're betting slips."

"Oh."

There didn't seem to be anything more to say. There was no jagged undercurrent of fear left in the room, no taint of horror as at the Dorsey crime scene. There was nothing, simply absence. Kate and Theo kept looking, standing side by side and staying quiet, as the sound of sirens became louder and eventually they heard the crunch of tires over the gravel outside.

THE BANK OF WHITEBOARDS IN the Incident room had grown. Two days after the discovery of Hargreaves' body, Kate and Olbeck stood in front of it, looking at the photographs from the victim's house. There was something even sadder in the juxtaposition of Hargreaves' slumped body, drained white, against the luxurious backdrop of the house itself, with its expensive furnishings and dramatic artwork. Kate looked more closely at a close-up shot of the suicide note. Something about it reminded her of the jagged letters written in blood on the wall of the dining room at the Dorsey crime scene. The handwriting and the meaning were completely different but, like the other, it was a message. But a message to whom?

The door crashed open and Anderton bowled through with a laptop in his arms, the lead trailing behind him like the ribbon on a kite.

"Morning, team. Can someone help me get this set up?"

Once the equipment was sorted out, the police officers arranged themselves around the room in a way that they could all see the projection screen. Anderton opened a file on the laptop and adjusted it on the screen. It was an Excel spreadsheet, filled side to side with a mass of (to Kate) impenetrable numbers.

"Know what this is?" asked Anderton.

Olbeck raised his hand. "I'm hazarding a guess that it's something to do with MedGen's accounts."

"You hazard right. We've had the analysts go through the files which were on the memory stick left by Hargreaves at his suicide. I'm not expecting you lot to understand this – you're not accountants, thank God – but you can possibly hazard another guess at why Hargreaves left this for us, or someone, to find."

Kate scanned the spreadsheets, frowning. The numbers still didn't make much sense, but she could guess what Anderton was inferring.

"He was embezzling funds," she said, quietly. "That's why Jack Dorsey was worried about money. Remember, Sarah Brennan said he'd been talking about getting the auditors in, to look at the accounts, or something like that?"

Anderton nodded. "Quite right, Kate. It turns out Alex Hargreaves not only had expensive tastes in houses and clothes and artwork, he also had quite a gambling addiction. Had accounts with all the bookies in Abbeyford, the respectable ones as well as the not-quite-so respectable ones. So he needed money and, as one of the directors of MedGen, he had access to a lot."

Kate found herself nodding in dawning comprehension. She remembered the trip to MedGen with Theo, how they'd been talking about betting and horse-racing in the waiting room. Theo holding the Racing Times magazine and Hargreaves coming in, noticing it, his face briefly registering a flicker of emotion. She remembered the bobbing pink betting slips in the lake by Hargreaves' house.

Olbeck rubbed his chin. "So, Hargreaves was taking the money, Dorsey found out about it – or was on the verge of finding out about it. So that meant... what? Did Hargreaves have to stop him?"

Theo was flipping the case notes back and forth. "Hargreaves has a rock-solid alibi for the night of Dorsey's death, guv," he said. "A pub full of people have confirmed that he was there for most of the evening."

"Yes, thank you for that illuminating fact, Theo," said Anderton. "I'm quite aware of that."

"He would make sure he had a rock-solid alibi if he was going to pay someone to do his dirty work for him," Kate said impatiently.

There was a moment's silence, broken by the door to the office opening. They all turned to see Stuart making his way towards them. He was dressed in his activist gear, in stark contrast to how Kate had last seen him, although he looked as tired as he had that evening at Olbeck and Jeff's house. He raised a hand in slightly self-conscious welcome as he joined them at the whiteboards. "All right, everyone?"

"Glad you could join us," said Anderton. "I hear the patrol had a fun time dragging you in for questioning."

Stuart grinned. "I didn't resist arrest, if that's what you're saying, sir."

"Not at all. Come into my office for a moment, I just want a quick word."

The tension in the team was broken as Anderton and Stuart left the room. Kate continued to run her eyes over the photographs and the files on screen, wondering whether she'd missed anything important. Theo took the files back to his desk and began to read through them, muttering something under his breath. Rav and Jane went to stock up on coffee.

Kate was still standing there, unsure of what to do next, when Stuart appeared at her shoulder. "All right?" he said amiably.

She smiled up at him in greeting. It was funny, but since that odd little moment at the dinner party last week, she didn't have that same sense of irritation and annoyance around him as she used to do.

"These the Hargreaves photos?"

Kate nodded. Stuart moved along the row slowly, looking at each in turn.

Kate, having seen all of the sad images that she wanted to see, looked around the room. Theo still had his head bent over the file – she could imagine that patronising little comment of Anderton's had smarted and he was trying to find something in the file to help him regain a little ground. She sympathised. She thought about going to get a cup of tea and turned back to Stuart to ask him if he wanted one. "Fancy a c—"

One look at his face stopped her sentence in mid-flow. He was staring intently at the photographs and his face was literally draining of colour before her eyes, as if a plug had been pulled somewhere in his throat and all the blood were running away down the plughole. She had a sudden, horrifying flashback to last summer, watching Gerry suffer the heart attack that put him in Intensive Care; here in front of her was the same greyish pallor, the same stare of utter shock and dread. She took an involuntary step towards him.

"Stuart..."

"Where are the toilets?" he asked, in a faint, faraway voice.

Surely he knew? She told him and he turned at once and walked quickly to the door, holding himself stiffly, as if he were hurt and trying not to show it. Kate watched the office door swing closed behind him, one hand up to her mouth. What on Earth...?

"Kate, can you come with me and—"

Olbeck had appeared at her shoulder. She turned to him and grasped his arm.

"Go and see if Stuart's all right, will you? He's in the men's loos."

"What?"

"Oh, never mind," said Kate impatiently and

hurried through the door after Stuart. Outside the grey painted door to the men's toilets, she hesitated for a second and then knocked and pushed it open.

Stuart was sitting on the floor of one of the cubicles, clearly oblivious to the filthy floor, his head in his hands. The room stank of vomit. Trying not to breathe, Kate squatted down by him and put a hand on his shoulder. "You all right?"

He raised his head and she saw with alarm that he was almost crying. "I'm fucked, Kate. I'm so fucked. Oh God, help me, I didn't know – I didn't know..."

She didn't waste time asking what was wrong. She had to get out of this fetid room but she couldn't leave Stuart. The door to the room opened and Olbeck walked in.

"What's the problem?" He caught sight of the state that was Stuart. "Oh, God. What's wrong?"

"Help me get him up."

They hoisted Stuart to his feet between them. He was crying openly now, and Olbeck looked across his bent head at Kate in alarm.

They manhandled him out of the loos and across into an empty office. Olbeck shut the door.

Stuart had his head in his hands again.

"What's going on?" asked Kate, gently.

There was no answer. She could hear Stuart's high, terrified breathing.

"Stuart!"

He dropped his hands from his face, rubbing the tears away. She could see him make an effort to collect himself. "I'm so *fucked*," he said, again.

"All right," said Olbeck. "Why?"

Stuart took a deep, shaky breath. "In the photos – the photos—"

"Of the Hargreaves crime scene?" asked Kate. She sat down next to him and took one of his large hands. He clutched it gratefully.

"Yeah, that scene. There's a sculpture in one of them, a big silver thing, a bit like a robot..."

"Yes?"

There was a moment's silence in the room, broken only by Stuart's ragged gasp. "I know who made it."

There was another silence. Kate and Olbeck exchanged a glance.

"Yes?" asked Kate, careful not to sound impatient. "And?"

Stuart put one shaky hand up to his eyes. "I know it – I know what happened. I can see the links now. I can see it all."

"So what happened?"

"I need to talk to Anderton. Oh Christ, he's going to kill me."

"Stuart," said Kate, fighting the impulse to take him by the shoulders and start shaking. "What the hell are you talking about?"

Stuart took a deep breath and got up, releasing

Kate's hand. He looked at her and then looked at Olbeck and smiled a smile that was nothing more than a grimace. "I've been fucking a murder suspect," he said and then walked out of the room, leaving Kate and Olbeck with their mouths ajar.

Chapter Twenty

THEY DIDN'T TALK MUCH IN the car on the way there. Rav was driving and Stuart sat next to him. Kate, who was by herself in the back, looked at Stuart's face, which was set tight, as if it had frozen stiff. She wished Anderton were there, or Olbeck, but they were both busy elsewhere and Stuart had specifically asked if she would accompany him.

"This is going to blow your cover," she'd said as they walked to the car. He'd laughed raggedly.

"You think that matters now? My career in Undercover is *over*, Kate. I'm probably off the force for good."

Kate thought of that grim note to his voice as he'd said that. She leaned forward and squeezed his arm. "Stuart, do you think – do you think this is a good idea? Should I make the arrest, instead?"

"No," said Stuart, that same note in his voice. "I want to see her face."

"Is it this turn?" asked Rav.

They swung off the main road into a cul-de-sac. The houses were pre-war; nineteen thirties construction, not particularly attractive but well-built and large, set back from the road with long driveways and front gardens. The house they sought was right on the edge of the estate, its boundary abutting a scrubby bit of woodland. Stuart, exiting the car, thought of the first time he'd been there and how he'd first seen her, spot lit under that harsh kitchen strip light.

The three of them stood for a moment, looking up at the silent house. There was a large, battered estate car parked on the crumbling concrete driveway that Stuart couldn't recall being there before. All the dirty curtains were drawn, although that wasn't so unusual, Stuart recalled. He wondered how many people were in the house.

"Well," said Rav. "What are we waiting for?"

"You're right," replied Stuart. "I'm going in."

There was a sharp crack and Kate felt the sudden sting of something in her upper arm and a buzzing noise. She looked down, expecting to see some kind of insect. Instead, there was a blooming patch of red on her bicep, the sleeve of her shirt torn open as if ripped by a tiny hand. She was still staring at this, the implications not reaching her brain quickly enough, when there was another crack and Rav gave a kind of grunt before folding up next to her, literally crumpling to the ground as if his legs had been dynamited from under him.

Within the next ten seconds, and how she didn't

know, she and Stuart were behind the parked car on the driveway, with Rav on the floor beneath them. She was still so dazed it took her a second to realise that she'd been shot, the bullet grazing her arm. Rav had been shot in the stomach. Had Stuart picked him up bodily whilst hurrying her under cover? She supposed he must have, but it was as if the last few moments of her memory had been burned away.

"What the fuck—"

"Shut up! Keep down!" said Stuart in a hissing shout. Kate heard Rav groan and dropped to her knees beside him. His face was an awful sepia tone, grey bleaching out the brown. He looked incredibly young. She put a hand on his chest and he clutched at her fingers. She had a sudden, piecing flash of memory; her brother Jay, when he was teething as a toddler. Kate, at eleven years old, would take him into her bed when he cried and he'd lie beside her, cuddled close, clutching her fingers. She did the same to Rav as she'd done then to Jay, lying close beside him and shielding him as best she could while she put her forehead against his clammy cheek and murmured to him just as she'd murmured to little Jay; *it's okay my darling, it's okay my sweetheart, you'll be okay...* She was conscious that any second could bring a final bullet to them both and the terror was so overwhelming that her comforting murmurs were as much for herself as for poor Rav. She was dimly aware that Stuart was pressed against her back, his arms around her, shielding her as she shielded Rav.

"It hurts, it hurts..." Rav moaned and Kate helplessly kissed his face and stroked his head, not knowing what else she could do. She daren't put any pressure on the wound, not knowing how badly his insides were injured. She had a vague recollection of Stuart shouting for an ARU, for an ambulance but that seemed a long time ago now. Was Rav dying, under her hands? Another shot pinged and ricocheted off the car and both Kate and Stuart flinched, huddling even closer to the ground.

"What's happening?" she asked Stuart, almost sobbing, as if he would know.

"I'm sorry, I'm sorry—"

His voice shook so much she almost couldn't make out the words. His arms tightened around her and she pressed back against him, feeling a tiny measure of comfort from his physical bulk.

Rav started to fit beneath her. She gasped and tried to hold him, feeling his muscles jerk and twitch beneath her hands. She tried to put her hands under his head to stop it banging on the concrete.

"Rav, oh hold on, hold on, sweetheart – hold on, darling – I've got you—"

She was crying properly now, her tears falling on Rav's grey face. *Don't die, oh please don't die...* Distantly, just as she had at Hargreaves's house, she heard the sound of sirens. Her heart leapt in hope within her.

"They're coming, Rav, they're nearly here, you'll be all right sweetheart, hold on..."

Then they heard it, even over the sound of the approaching emergency vehicles. There another shot but from within the house, a gunshot that somehow sounded more final than any of the ones before. Stuart and Kate remained frozen for a second. Had they heard what they thought they'd heard? Rav calmed and his body stilled beneath Kate's hands. Terrified, she bent to put her head on his chest and exhaled sharply in relief, not even knowing she had been holding her breath, as she heard his heartbeat beneath her ear, faint and erratic but there all the same.

"What was that?"

"I don't know. Don't move. Don't do anything until the ARU get here."

All the cars and teams seemed to arrive at once .There was a confusion of screeching tyres, shouts, blue lights pulsing, running feet, more shouts. Kate stayed crouched down, her arms around Rav, until she was pushed aside by a paramedic, a burly middle-aged man with a beard. She fought the urge to kiss him. Almost before she could say anything, another female paramedic crouched beside her, talking calmly but forcefully.

"Officer, are you hurt? Are you shot? Can you tell me?"

"I'm fine, I'm fine." Kate looked around, dazed.

Rav was being loaded onto a stretcher, the bearded medic bent over him. Where was Stuart? Was it safe to sit up?

"That arm looks nasty, I'll have to treat that."

Ignoring her, Kate flung herself floorwards again and looked across the driveway from beneath the car. She could see a semi-circle of police cars, several armed officers with their guns trained on the house. Almost as she looked, she heard the front door go down with a splintering crash amidst shouts of "Armed police! Armed police!"

"Officer, you need to come with me for a moment. We'll be safe over here..."

The female para was gently pulling her away to the shelter of an ambulance, parked behind the fence that marked the boundary. Kate craned her neck, trying to see where Stuart was. Had he gone inside?

"Officer, *please*. You need to come with me."

Another ambulance's siren started up, loud enough to make Kate jump. She watched it drive away, bearing Rav with it. She muttered a quick, open-eyed prayer as she watched its tail-lights recede into the distance. Please God, let him be okay...

"Officer—"

Kate relented. She followed the paramedic into the remaining ambulance and allowed them to shut the door.

Stuart stepped through the broken front door frame of the house. Fragments of wood lay scattered across the hallway's dirty floor tiles. ARU officers thronged the rooms downstairs. In so far as he was able to wonder about anything, Stuart wondered whether anyone else had been in the house – that curly-haired Charlie, or the one with the funny name, Rizzo or something. He hoped not.

He climbed the stairs, watching the treads move in and out of his vision. His chest ached and his jaw; he'd been clenching it for so long. Up to the first floor, where rooms had been checked and cleared. He paused at the beginning of the final staircase. How strange that he was climbing upwards when his life was in an uncontrollable spiral downwards. There was no escape now, nothing to stop his descent. He walked slowly up the narrow wooden stairs, hand desperately clutching the banister. The door at the top of the stairs was open, leaning drunkenly on its hinges. They'd broken that one down, too. There were two uniformed officers by the doorway, staring into the room. As Stuart approached them, one turned to him and said something, but he was too far gone now to understand. He moved into the room of glittering mirrors and again, he was reminded of the first time he'd been there. Again, he watched himself in miniature, a million tiny reflections of himself, a million tiny images of his haggard, aghast face.

The body of Guy Ward lay face down on the floor, one side of his head a ragged mess of blood and bone. A shotgun lay by one outstretched hand and there was another gun lying on the floor between the body and the bed. Angie was stretched out on the bed with two officers restraining her, pinning her to its surface. For a frozen moment, Stuart thought she was dead too and then realised her face was turned towards him, her eyes fixed on him, unblinking. She wasn't struggling. He looked once at her beautiful statue's face and then his gaze rose to the large computer screen on the desk by the wall. He swallowed.

There was the Dorsey drawing room, the beautiful antiques, the velvet curtains. For a moment, Stuart thought he was looking at a photograph of the room and then there was a flicker in the corner of the screen and he watched Wade advance on Jack Dorsey, who was turning, open-mouthed. Where was Angie? Behind the camera; he answered his own question a second later. Stuart watched up until the moment the knife first went in and then he looked away, feeling sick. He remembered Angie showing him that other multi-media collage on her phone – the same time he'd seen her silver sculpture. Was this to have been her next project? A living snuff film, if that wasn't a contradiction in terms. He had to get out of this room. He remembered her telling him about her latest artwork. *It's consumed me...*

Anger and nausea rose up in him and, to stop himself from attacking her even as she lay prone and flattened on the bed, he rushed for the door. The walls flickered, a million little Stuarts running with him.

Chapter Twenty One

WHEN KATE HAD FINALLY GOT back to the incident room, Olbeck had said nothing but simply thrown his arms around her and held her tight for a long time. Then he'd stepped back and touched the bandage on her upper arm. He'd traced a line across from the bandage to the centre of her chest. "God, if that had been four inches further across..."

"Oy, hands off the boobs," Kate had said.

"Well, it's the only pair I'm ever likely to get my hands on," Olbeck had replied. Then his mouth had twisted and he'd pulled her back into a hug.

It was seven thirty in the morning, the day after the shooting, and they were all waiting, pacing the floors, biting their nails, drinking cup after cup of the rank instant coffee that was all the station could offer. Most of the team hadn't slept at all. They were all fixated on the door and when it finally crashed back, admitting Anderton, there was an audible intake of breath heard.

He didn't waste time keeping them in suspense. "He's alive, he's okay," said Anderton.

That in-held breath rushed out. Jane burst into noisy tears, sobbing, "Sorry – sorry, everyone," and then cried again. Theo put his arm around her and she leaned into him, hiding her face. Kate sat down suddenly, the nervous energy that had propelled her through the rest of the night suddenly dissipating. Olbeck sat down next to her and put his head in his hands for a moment, rubbing his eyes. Kate heard him murmur something like *oh, thank God*.

Anderton's eyes were pouched with shadow and his skin had that grey tinge of exhaustion. He held up a hand. "I should qualify that a bit. Rav's not *okay*, he's very badly hurt. But he'll live. I know you're all dying to see him, but he's in Intensive Care. He's not allowed visitors at the moment and obviously his parents and his sisters will be first in the queue when he is, all right?"

They all nodded. Jane wiped her face and sat back up again.

Kate opened her mouth to ask about Stuart, and then shut it again. She had a feeling she wouldn't like the answer.

"Now," said Anderton. "Now, those who want to can go home and get some sleep. I've got our prime suspect to interview. Anyone want to sit in on that with me?"

"I will," Kate said, immediately.

"Me too," said Olbeck.

Theo opened his mouth for a second and then shut it again.

"Right," said Anderton. "Let's go then."

THE WOMAN'S FACE REMINDED KATE of a statue, one of those ancient marble Greek sculptures. The same strong lines of the face, the same absence of expression. The woman's eyes had that same blankness, too. She was beautiful but it was the beauty of a distant supernova or the sinuous curves of a poisonous snake; something lethal, best appreciated at a distance.

Too fanciful, Kate. She turned her attention back to Anderton and what he was saying.

"So, Angie," said Anderton, pleasantly. "We've been having a look at your records. What made you choose the name Angela Sangello?"

Angie looked at him with no expression. "She's an Italian artist of the twentieth century," she said, in a bored tone. "Don't worry. *You* won't have heard of her."

"I'm afraid I haven't. But then I don't know much about art."

The contempt in Angie's face was now visible. Kate clamped down on a smile. She knew Anderton had a variety of ways of softening up a suspect and knew that his line in self-deprecation would be just the thing to get through to this arrogant, chilly girl.

"That's not your real name, is it though?" asked Anderton. "Not according to our records. You were born Clara King, firstborn daughter of Damien King, or should I say Lord King, hereditary peer. Ring any bells?"

"I'm estranged from my family," said Angie, coldly.

"How very sad. I wonder why that could be?"

Angie remained silent.

"Now, let me see, your mother died when you were seven. I'm sorry. And your father married again when you were ten. Am I right, so far?"

The solicitor next to Angie, a grey-haired, middle-aged man, shifted slightly in his seat. No doubt he, as well as Angie, was wondering where this was going.

"Now, your new stepmother and father had another child, didn't they? Another girl. Can you tell me anything about your sister, Angie? Or should I call you Clara?"

Angie's face tightened a little, but she still said nothing. Anderton continued.

"Now, it seems that your younger sister was tragically killed in an accident when she was two. She fell from the top of a quarry near your house at the time, near Guildford. What an awful thing. That must have been extremely traumatic for the family. Was it very traumatic, Angie?"

Angie's face had settled back into blankness. She didn't respond to Anderton's question.

"Now, it seems that after this dreadful event, your father actually had you taken into care. Why was that? Could you not cope with your sister's death?"

Angie looked at him with contempt. "My stepmother hated me. She was just looking for an excuse to get rid of me."

"Oh, is that why?" Anderton shuffled the papers before him into a little more order. He went on, the gentleness of his tone belying the devastation of his words. "It wasn't because your father and your stepmother thought you were actually responsible for your sister's death?"

The solicitor made a sound of protest but Angie cut across him. "You can think that, if you like," she said, her eyes narrowed. "I don't give a shit. If you've got access to my notes, you'll see there was no charge."

"No, that's true, that's true," said Anderton. "There was no actual *charge*. Father pulled some strings, did he? Or was it that he knew, deep down, exactly what his daughter was, but just couldn't face up to it?"

Angie scoffed. She leaned back in her chair, looking away ostentatiously.

"Well," continued Anderton. "We've also had a look at your medical notes. Diagnosed with a personality disorder at sixteen, I see. In and out of various therapies, expelled from your boarding school…"

He waited a moment.

"What I find remarkable," he said, in the same quiet tone, "is that you've managed to make such a name for yourself, despite such, well, difficult beginnings. Your art, your relationships… quite remarkable. And it helps that you're beautiful, too. That must really help."

Kate kept her face neutral as he elaborated on this theme for some minutes. It was working, though. She could see Angie gradually thawing, becoming more animated. The more Anderton heaped praise upon her, the more she responded. Anderton had a lot of charm, when he wanted to use it – God knows, Kate knew about *that* – and he was laying it on thick, here.

"So," said Anderton eventually, smiling genially. "How did you and Alex Hargreaves meet?"

Angie fell into his trap. "At a poker game," she said. Then she smiled and laughed a little cruelly. "I thrashed him. Alex was obsessed with gambling - shame he wasn't any good at it."

"He was an admirer of your work?"

"Of course."

"And you were lovers?"

Angie's smile dimmed a little. "Occasionally."

"So, you wouldn't say it was a serious relationship?"

"No, not really."

"I see," said Anderton. "Well, that's strange. We've been going through his personal belongings and he seems to have all sorts of pictures of you, including several obviously taken at social events. If we asked Alex's friends, do you think they might give us a different answer?"

Angie shrugged, seemingly unconcerned. "They might. It depends what he told them. He was always much more keen on the relationship than I was."

"Is that right?"

"Yes," Angie said. Her gaze slid from Anderton's face to come to rest on Kate's. "You know what men are like."

Angie smiled a slow smile directed at Kate, her eyelids falling slightly. For a moment Kate, incredibly, felt it – whatever had snagged Stuart, and Wade, and Alexander Hargreaves. She found herself smiling back, leaning forward, almost eagerly. Shocked at herself, she sat back sharply in her chair and snapped the smile from her face. Angie's smile changed, from conspiratorial to triumphant. Kate thought of those Sirens from Greek mythology, who'd lured sailors to their deaths by their sweet singing. I need to stop my ears with wax, she thought.

"Did you know that Alexander Hargreaves was embezzling funds from his company, MedGen?"

Angie's eyes widened. "No," she said and Kate could have congratulated her on the feigned shock in her voice. For the first time since the arrest, Kate started to think that perhaps they might have bitten off more than they could chew.

"You had no idea?"

"Of course not."

"Did he ask you for help in any way?"

Angie looked at him coolly. "I have no idea what you mean."

"You didn't introduce Alex Hargreaves to your other lover, Guy Wade? They didn't arrange the killing of Jack Dorsey between them?"

Angie was shaking her head, seemingly horrified. "I don't know what you're talking about. Guy was – Guy was a brutal man. I was terrified for my life."

Anderton sat back and regarded her. She looked at him, her eyes big and dark. "So, tell me what really happened, Angie," he said, softly.

The silence stretched on and on. Kate could even hear the faint ticking of the clock up on the wall, an ancient model which hadn't yet been replaced by a digital one. From outside, came the sounds of normal life; car engines, bird song, slamming doors.

"Well," said Anderton eventually, seeing Angie wasn't going to speak. "Here's what I think happened. Perhaps you'll correct me if I'm wrong."

Silence. Angie's face had changed again, from a beautiful stony mask, to the hurt expression of a young vulnerable girl. Oh, she was good – Kate would give her that.

"You and Alex Hargreaves were lovers. You were also the lover of Guy Wade, a violent and revengeful animal rights militant. How did you meet him, by the way?" Anderton waited a second for Angie to answer and then went on, clearly knowing she wouldn't. "You made a piece of art for him, Angie, didn't you? The multi-media piece, with the footage of all the animal cruelty? What made you decide to go even further? Was it his idea, or yours, to film the death of Jack Dorsey?"

Angie's face had stilled again. Kate could see a distant spark in the depths of her dark eyes, as if her thoughts were there, ticking over, the only outward sign of her search looking for a plausible explanation. When she spoke, it sounded as though it was something she'd been preparing for some time. No doubt, she had.

"Guy threatened me," she said. Her voice quavered a little and Kate inwardly cursed, knowing the effect that would have on a jury. "He was obsessed with animal cruelty. He said if I didn't help him, he'd *kill* me. You have to believe me."

"So what did he ask you to do? Did he plant the bomb that killed Michael Frank?"

Angie nodded, her head down.

"Did you help him with that?"

"No."

Kate spoke up, unable to help herself. "Did you *film* it?"

Angie looked at her and for a moment, Kate saw the snake, down there in the darkness, stirring. "No."

"Really?" said Kate sceptically. "So I guess when we wade through all the footage on your computer, Angie, we won't find anything like that? I wonder."

Angie's mouth tightened a little and Kate felt a little spark of triumph. She was pretty sure that once they'd searched through all the evidence, they would find exactly that.

Anderton gave her a glance and she sat back, letting him take up the reins.

"You're a pretty persuasive person, Angie, from all I've heard. Men become quite obsessed with you, don't they? Did you suggest to Alex Hargreaves that you could introduce him to someone who could do his dirty work for him?" Angie said nothing, staring at him blankly. "Did you suggest to Guy Wade that you could give him access to one of his targets?"

"I don't know what you're talking about," said Angie, coldly.

"No? How did Guy Wade know the alarm codes to Jack Dorsey's home? How did he know where Jack Dorsey's home was? How did he know to locate and wipe the CCTV onsite?"

Angie shrugged.

"He knew, Angie, because you told him. Hargreaves told you, and you passed the information on to Wade. You were there at the scene, holding the camera, Angie. And, in fact, I think you were the way in. Darryl Timms opened the door to you because you were no threat, were you, Angie? Is that right? He saw a frightened, tiny young girl on the doorstep and opened the door to you. That's why he was facing away from the door when he was killed, because he was leading you into the house. That's when your lover, Guy Wade, came up behind him and killed him."

Angie crossed her arms across herself. "I was being *threatened*," she said, as if Anderton was unbelievably dense. "Guy told me he'd kill me if I didn't do what he said. He *forced* me. He forced me to film it."

"Well," said Anderton. "As he's dead, we can't really ask him, can we? How did he die, Angie?"

She stared back at him. "He shot himself in the head."

"Did he? You didn't shoot him yourself?"

"There's no evidence of that," interjected the solicitor, sharply.

"Exactly," said Angie. She flashed Anderton a tight smile. "I was being held *hostage*, in case you'd forgotten."

"When the officers who were first on the scene

found you, you were sitting calmly at your editing suite, working on the footage of Jack Dorsey's murder. Does that sound like someone who was in terror for their life?"

"I told you, I wasn't in my right mind, I was terrified. I can't account for every single thing I was doing."

Anderton sat back in his chair. "Forensics can tell us a lot, Angie. I wonder what we'll find on the gun that killed Guy Wade? Your fingerprints overlaying his, perhaps?"

There was a beat of silence. Then Angie raised her head a little, turning her face so it could be clearly seen by the recording camera. Her mouth quivered.

"I moved the gun after he was dead," she said, almost choking the words out. "I was so frightened he wasn't dead and he was going to get up and kill me."

With half his head missing? Kate held down a cough of disbelief. The trouble was, Angie's performance was all too convincing. She was aware of a slowly creeping unease, a discordant note, something that they'd missed.

It didn't take long to surface. The grey-haired solicitor stirred himself, pulling himself upright.

"Am I to understand, Chief Inspector, that my client is being held on suspicion of murder? I see nothing you've put forward in this interview to show that my client can be held responsible for any of the terrible crimes you seem to be accusing her of. There is simply no justification for holding her on this charge."

"I can hold her on plenty more," snapped Anderton. He pushed his chair back from the table. Both Angie and the solicitor regarded him; the solicitor with a cynical smile and Angie with the same hurt, vulnerable look she'd worn before. Kate's palm itched to slap her.

"A short break," said Anderton. "I'll leave you to confer with Miss Sangello. Or should that be Miss King?"

He, Kate and Olbeck huddled in the corridor, far enough away so their whispered conversation couldn't be overheard.

"Fuck," said Anderton. "I was hoping he wouldn't pick up on that."

"You're joking, right?" said Kate. "We can't hold her on a murder charge?"

"Look, I'm doing my best, here. But we've got no evidence that she had anything to do with the car bomb – yes, there might be footage, but all she needs to say was what she's been saying about the Dorsey case. She did it under duress. We actually have the murder of Jack Dorsey *on tape* – it's irrefutably Wade."

Kate's chest felt tight. "What about Wade?

Surely we can prove that she handled the gun. The angle, the fingerprints..."

Anderton half smiled. "Well, you see how quickly she threw out an excuse for having her prints on the gun. We can pin our hopes on forensics, but..." He shrugged.

Olbeck put both hands up to his temples as if he had a sudden headache. "You're not telling me this – this sociopath – is going to just walk away?"

Both Anderton and Kate gave him an old-fashioned look.

"How many years have you been a detective, Mark?" said Anderton. "For Christ's sake, she's not getting off scot free. She's an accessory to murder, for one thing. Concealing a crime. There's plenty there to be going on with—"

"But not what she's truly guilty of," Kate said, quietly.

The three of them stared at each other for a moment.

"Look, let's not go giving up yet," said Anderton. "We've got hundreds of pieces of evidence to go through. There'll be something there that can help. And even if there isn't..." he trailed off for a second. "Something will come up. You'll see."

They walked back into the interview room together. Anderton conferred with the solicitor, letting him know with a kind of quiet intensity that they would be detaining Angie for further questioning, murder charge or not. The solicitor nodded a crisp assent and briefly murmured in Angie's ear. Kate watched her face closely but the stony mask had slipped back down again.

Kate waited until Anderton had left the room. Olbeck was preparing to leave. She flashed him a quick glance and then walked over to the table. Angie looked at her sullenly.

"Oh, and by the way," said Kate, quietly. "You're not an artist."

Angie said nothing for a moment. Then, frowning, she opened her mouth to reply.

"Yes, I—"

"You're not, you know," Kate went on, cutting her off. "Artists create. That's what they do. You don't create, you destroy. You're not an artist."

Angie's face contracted. Now, as Angie's pupils shrank down to tiny, glittering pinpoints of fury, Kate was reminded of another figure from Greek mythology. *Medusa.* If looks could kill... but Kate knew she'd got through. The barb had struck home. That's for Stuart, you bitch – and Mary, and Madeline, and Harriet, and Jack, and the children. Take that. The solicitor was looking at her with a look she couldn't decipher, his mouth slightly twisted. Inside her, she felt a delicious leap of self-righteous glee.

Kate stepped back. "Yes," she said, infusing her tone with just a hint of pity. "You're *not* an artist.

You might want to mull that thought over, in prison. You'll have a nice long time to really think it through."

Behind her, Olbeck stifled a laugh. Kate kept her face in the same rueful, pitying smile and she didn't clench her fist in triumph until they were both safely out of the room.

"Nice one," said Olbeck, as they reached the corridor. "I'm only surprised you didn't cough 'whole life term' under your breath as you left the room."

"I would have done, if I'd thought about it."

They both looked at each other and collapsed, bellowing slightly hysterical laughter. Kate knew Angie would be able to hear them from inside the room. *Good.*

They walked back to the office, half-supporting one another, still wheezing. Theo looked up in surprise as they staggered through the door.

"What's up with you two?"

"Oh, nothing," Kate said, wiping her eyes. "Just a bit of a delayed reaction, I think."

"Right," Theo said, in a mystified tone. "Anyway, I've got some good news. Madeline Dorsey's regained consciousness."

Kate and Olbeck looked at each other, sobering up completely.

"That's brilliant," said Olbeck. He sat down at

a nearby desk, running his hands through his hair. "That's great. Do they think she'll recover?"

"As far as I could tell. They were being cautious, but I gather that's the gist."

"Fantastic," Kate said. She pinched her nose and heaved a deep sigh. "What did Anderton say? Something will turn up."

"Well—" Olbeck began.

"Come on, this could be it! Hopefully all the additional evidence we'll need."

Olbeck looked sombre. "Come on, Kate. You know as well as I do that she might not be able to remember a thing. Traumatic amnesia and all that."

"Yeah," said Theo. "We might very well end up with nothing."

"Oh, I know." Kate reached out and shook them both gently, one hand on each. "But let's hope for the best, eh?"

The two men smiled reluctantly.

Kate went back to her desk to collect her bag and coat. She was so tired that even moving felt like wading through slowly setting concrete. She dropped her head on her desk and sighed.

Olbeck paused on his way past. "Are you all right, really?"

Kate nodded, head still down. Then, with an effort, she lifted it.

"I'm all right," she said. "You know what? I was

just thinking I might have a pop at the Inspector's exams."

"Why not? You'll breeze through them, I'm sure."

"I'm sure I will," said Kate. "After all, if *you* can pass them..."

Olbeck snorted and Kate grinned tiredly.

On the steps of the station, Kate felt her phone vibrate. Another message from Andrew, to add to the multiple calls that she'd let go to voicemail. Standing there in the sunshine, too exhausted for her usual denial to kick in, Kate faced the fact. She didn't love him. Surely the first person you'd normally want to see after a traumatic experience would be your boyfriend? She didn't want to see him; all she wanted to do was go home, on her own. Olbeck passed her with a pat on the shoulder – she could see Jeff in the car down on the road, waiting to collect him. That was what a relationship should be. You know it, Kate. You know what you have to do.

She sighed a little.

"You all right?" asked Theo, passing her.

"I'm fine." When were people going to stop asking her that?

"Need a lift home?"

She smiled at him. He was a good lad, really. "Yes. Please. Thanks, Theo."

As she got into his car, she sent Andrew a text.

I'll call you later and tell you everything. Don't worry. She didn't put a kiss on the end of it.

THE END

ENJOYED THIS BOOK? AN HONEST review left at Amazon, Goodreads, Shelfari and LibraryThing is always welcome and *really* important for indie authors. The more reviews an independently published book has, the easier it is to market it and find new readers.

Sign up to Celina Grace's newsletter here at her website http://www.celinagrace.com for news of new releases, promotions and other goodies. You can unsubscribe at any time and won't be bombarded with emails, promise!

WANT MORE Kate Redman?

THE NEW KATE REDMAN MYSTERY, **Chimera**, is now available on Amazon...

ABBEYFORD IS CELEBRATING ITS ANNUAL pagan festival, when the festivities are interrupted by the discovery of a very decomposed body. Soon, several other bodies are discovered but is it a question of foul play or are these deaths from natural causes? It's a puzzle that DS Kate Redman and the team could do without, caught up as they are in investigating an unusual series of robberies. Newly single again, Kate also has to cope with her upcoming Inspector exams and a startling announcement from her friend and colleague DI Mark Olbeck...

When a robbery goes horribly wrong, Kate begins to realise that the two cases might be linked. She must use all her experience and intelligence to solve a series of truly baffling crimes which bring her up against an old adversary from her past...

ACKNOWLEDGEMENTS

MANY THANKS TO ALL THE following splendid souls:

Chris Howard for the brilliant cover designs; Andrea Harding for editing and proofreading; Kathy McConnell for extra proofreading and beta reading; lifelong Schlockers and friends David Hall, Ben Robinson and Alberto Lopez; Ross McConnell for advice on police procedural and for also being a great brother; Kathleen and Pat McConnell, Anthony Alcock, Naomi White, Mo Argyle, Lee Benjamin, Bonnie Wede, Sherry and Amali Stoute, Cheryl Lucas, Georgia Lucas-Going, Steven Lucas, Loletha Stoute and Harry Lucas, Helen Parfect, Helen Watson, Emily Way, Sandy Hall, Kristýna Vosecká; and of course my patient and ever-loving Chris, Mabel, Jethro and Isaiah.

This book is for Chris, with all my love.

83624879R00152

Made in the USA
Columbia, SC
11 December 2017